Sarah Comes out Swinging

SARAH MONROE MYSTERIES

Sarah Comes Out Swinging

Sarah Rolling with the Punches

Sarah Takes a Stand

Sarah Here We Go Again

Sarah Blood Runs Downhill

Sarah Things Are Not as They Seem

For Katie, I hope you dance.

Chapter 1

My heart was pounding as I realized I was sitting up. I could hear a low growl come from Maggie on the end of the bed. I tried to get my eyes accustomed to the dark as I frantically looked around. What was going on? What did she hear? I listened but all I could hear was my heart pounding.

I couldn't really figure out what was going on …as my mind raced over the last day's events…. I was glad I had made the move…the mountains of Montana had gotten cold and had too many memories. I needed to leave my past behind and start fresh, somewhere warm where I could work on my books and not really think, well at least not of the past.

I'm a mystery writer. My agent was all for the move. Raeghen pushed me when needed, usually about my manuscripts, but now I needed a life push. I had taken too much time off; my head was a little cloudy. so a fresh start seemed to be the thing.

I picked a small town in Michigan by the lake, the pier was beautiful. Actually I purchased a place outside of downtown, sight unseen off the Internet. The pictures of the town looked beautiful with cobblestone streets and a hometown look but best of all nobody knew me.

While it had warm weather for most of the year it still had its spot of cold…so I wouldn't miss the mountains too much. Raeghen either called me from New York or emailed so the location would not matter to her…as long as I could get my drafts for my book to her on time and it was time I finished the
one I had been working on.

As I unpacked boxes...I looked around the room. I had been successful with my mystery books and that had allowed me a comfortable living and the funds to purchase this lovely, comfortable cottage. It had 3 bedrooms.

One I used for my office, which also accommodated a Futon. I loved the room because of the large window overlooking the lake, my bedroom I slept in, and a regular guest room. All three were very nice.

It had a very comfortable living room, a small dining room and a nice bright kitchen. The selling point was the screened in back porch that overlooked Lake Michigan. The large fenced backyard sloped down with a gate at the bottom opening onto the beach. Right outside the screened in porch was a large patio with a picnic table and area for a grill. There was a small shed that held the lawn mower and chairs also.

To the right of my house there were a couple of small homes and a large resort of A Frames for tourists. To the left more beach and beautiful homes on the bluff. Big trees graced my front yard. I felt like I could just hide away, comfortable and private.

I never learned to swim, in fact I was afraid of water, but here, here I wanted to "expand my horizons" as my friend Hannah would tell me. Maybe I would learn to swim and boat. Hannah had always been my cheerleader and got me through a lot the last couple of years. She was my "person"; a friend who knows you better than anyone and just "gets you." She was all for the move although there was now distance between us but there were phones and always planes that went both ways. We set up Skype on our computers so we were always in touch... and for now she would be coming this way when I got settled. Maggie needed a yard...and had made herself quite at home chasing birds in it and hunting, well whatever dogs hunt
. Maggie had been with me for the last five years. She was a German Wired Haired dog that was so loving yet very protective, even more so since, well since Montana.

She seemed to know what I thought. The thing about dogs…they accept you for who you are, always happy to see you and Mags was always up for a walk. And right now she wanted a walk.

"First we eat." I told her. My stomach had been growling for the last hour so it was time. I stopped unpacking and got a baguette out of the cupboard.
 Slicing it in half and then lengthwise, I put some pizza sauce on them and chopped ham, green peppers, mushrooms, sauerkraut with cheddar and mozzarella.

 Sticking the pan in the oven, I went in to change in to some shorts and pulled my long thick, black hair into a ponytail and put on some jogging shoes. Maybe I would start running again on a regular basis again, something to think about.

 The pizza bread was bubbly when I went back to the kitchen. Maggie had two pieces, which she promptly gobbled up, and I had two. She licked her lips with approval. Now that we were full I grabbed the leash. Locking the door, we went down the path onto the quiet street.

It was a nice quiet neighborhood. The houses or cottages as some of them were, seemed well kept. I hadn't met my neighbors yet, not that they didn't try. There were a couple of times they knocked on the door, probably to welcome us, but I didn't think I was quite ready to have to explain who I was, why I moved, well anyway, I didn't answer the door. Maggie certainly let them know I didn't live alone. But they say time heals wounds so here I was.

As I started out on the street I didn't go far when I noticed a woman across the street out in her yard working in her flowers. Maggie never met a stranger she didn't like…well maybe a few. This lady had a wide brimmed straw hat on, not that that was unusual but it was bright orange. Maybe that's what caught Maggie's interest.

And while that hat was wide, covering up most of her face it was her talking that caught my interest…she was talking to the flowers like they were children…" Come on you little ones perk up and let's have some fun in the sun." I smiled to myself at the sight. She stood up and looked our way and waved. I raised my hand to return the wave and walk by but Maggie had other ideas. She jerked the leash out of my hand and off she ran in the direction of Hat Lady. She ran up to her and as she snuggled with her, Hat Lady scratched her ears just where she like it. She had some kind of dog experience here.

Then I heard it…a little bark here and there and a bunch of snorting and out from under a bush came two pugs!
One was, well he was enormous and the other one was quite small…. Maggie instantly became friends. Rolling on the ground and playing with them they chased each other. Not so sure I was as ready to become acquainted with their owner yet, but I found I had no choice.

Hat Lady took off her garden glove and extended her hand. "So nice to meet you dear, I'm Martha Lane and these are my pugs. Monty is the king sized pug and the other is Tilly. Would you like to stop and have a glass of cool lemonade?"

Before I could answer she kept on "I have a pitcher freshly made and we can sit on the patio in the shade out of the heat so the boys and girls can play. Now what is your furry friend's name?" she nodded to Mags.

"Maggie" I replied and off she went walking. I guess I was supposed to follow so I did, around the side of the house and back to the patio, which was even lovelier than the front yard. There was a table and chairs and the back yard was breathtaking! Flowers everywhere!

Brilliant yellows, oranges, reds, and purples… the colors went on and on. It was such a lovely surprise, and I commented as much. There was a small brick walkway that wound through this maze of colors and well, it was amazing.

"Sit down dear, and rest for a while in this heat!" Mrs. Lane said and sat herself down promptly. She poured a glass of lemonade for each of us and I sipped wonderful, icy, cool lemonade. As I got a better look at Hat Lady aka Mrs. Lane, I instantly thought I would like her. She had a beautiful smile and soft, warm eyes.

Her gray hair peeked out from under the hat, which she was now taking off. It wasn't so much her looks but the way she greeted me, as if we were old friends getting together again for a visit. I was instantly at ease.

"So have you unpacked and gotten comfortable in your new home? "she asked. "Well I'm trying, unpacking seems to take a while." I replied.

"Of course, but you will enjoy yourself when it's all done. The Lake is a beautiful spot. You will meet everyone as time goes by.

The couple next to you just moved in a few days before you and on the other side of you is someone, I'm not sure who, but they are a bit of a recluse I think." She said. No questions for me; I was surprised and curious.

Usually people want to know everything about you, where you came from, what you do for a living, but Hat Lady wanted no information. I was surprised I was so relaxed and comfortable sitting in this beautiful backyard sipping lemonade on a hot day like we were old friends.

"Have you lived here long Mrs. Lane?" I asked. "Oh yes dear!" she replied. My late husband Todd and I bought this house when we were first married and raised our children here. We were so happy and had such fun times by this lake. Now they are all raised and gone, as well as my Todd. He passed 4 years ago."

"Oh, I'm sorry." I said. "Oh no dear, don't worry, when the Lord see fit to take away He always gives you more, maybe in a different way, but HE helps you through it." I wanted to argue that point but remembered what my mom would always tell me.

"Sarah, God has a plan for you, it's gona be great, it's gona be wild and it's gona be full of HIM!" Not sure I could see that plan right now.

I kept quiet as she continued. "I keep very busy. I'm very active in my church, and I volunteer at the local dog pound. I'm actually a foster mom for dogs when they don't have enough room to house them all. That's where these two came from.
" She said pointing to Monty and Tilly who now had Maggie down on the ground and were climbing on top of her to her delight.
"Their owner moved to take a new job and couldn't take them with him, so now they have a home with me. Your Maggie is welcome any time to come here and play. And of course I garden as you can see and I'm an avid book reader.
My girls got me a kindle last year and I have read so many books on it. Do you like to read dear?" she asked.

"Well actually, I'm a writer." I replied instantly regretting giving out the information.
But I didn't have to worry, as Mrs. Lane didn't pry. "How nice dear, then you can do your work from your new home and relax!" she said. I nodded in agreement thinking I really like her. We visited a while longer, mostly about her flowers and then I stood up.

"Well, we should be going. I still have a lot of boxes to go through." I said. "Of course you do, but I'm so glad you stopped by. I always have coffee on in the morning and when it's hot out you're more than welcome to have another glass of lemonade with me," she said with a smile.

"Thank you, I appreciate that, and thank you for the lemonade, it was delicious." I replied as I turned to leave and pry Mags out from underneath the pugs. "By the way, my name is Sarah." I said. "It's really been nice to meet you Sarah, stop by anytime and enjoy the rest of your walk." Mrs. Lane said and smiled.

I had to literally drag Maggie away from her new playmates as they barked and snorted a chorus of goodbyes. So now she had friends as well as I did. We continued on and I found I had a smile on my face. This might not be too bad a place to live. Mrs. Lane seemed very friendly and not prying, and should I find myself too lonely I could wander down to her place. I'm sure Monty and Tilly would love to see Maggie.

As I walked, I passed a large house on the left of mine, with a large lot separating us. It seemed quite a lot larger than the other houses in the neighborhood. It was brick and two stories with a tall black iron fence around it. It seemed, well, not at all inviting like the other houses. The yard was a little overgrown, not well kept like the rest of the neighborhood seemed to be.

Movement caught my eye from one of the upstairs windows, but I couldn't see anyone. It intrigued me as I walked by, maybe an idea for another book? I would have to ask Mrs. Lane about it next time I visited. Just past the brick house a little way down the road, I decided to turn around. As we stopped I looked up and noticed another house sitting back in the trees. It was a neat well-kept ranch style house. I noticed it because it was red and I liked it the instant I saw it.

It had an attached garage and the garage door was open. There was a tan truck with the hood up as if someone had been working on it. I stood in the middle of the road just staring; trying to imagine who lived there.

The yard was well kept and I noticed a large motorcycle in the garage. As I stood there staring someone looked up from underneath the hood of the truck. I was instantly embarrassed but couldn't move as I surveyed what I saw. The man was in his middle thirties I'd say, tall, dark tan and beautiful black hair. He seemed well fit from the looks of him. He was dressed in a pair of blue jeans and burnt orange T-shirt. He just looked at me, not annoyed, just looked.

I jerked out of my daydream and pulled Maggie. "Come on Mags lets go." I walked quickly back in the direction of my house, now in a hurry to get home. My cell rang as we continued on
. "Sarah how is it going, are you unpacked yet?" Raeghen asked as I held the phone to my ear. "Hey girl, just checking up on my best writer. Are you getting settled?" she asked.

Actually, Mags and I are on a walk. We did meet one of my neighbors." I said into the phone. "Great Sarah!!! That's great. You need to get out and back into life and the world. Any new men on the scene?" asked Raeghen.

"Now Raeghen, you know how I feel." I said just a little agitated. "Sarah," she began, "it's been a little over a year hon and life goes on. I just want you to be happy again." Raeghen replied and I knew she meant it. "No." I said. "You just want me to finish my book!" I kidded her. "You know better." Raeghen replied. "OK girl, I have another call coming in so I'll call you later. Love you!" and she hung up.

As I walked, I thought about Raeghen and how she was more than just my agent. I shut down emotionally when Caleb was killed and she was there for me as well as my friend Hannah. As I thought about the past I still felt that lump in my throat. I never thought I would meet anyone as loving as Caleb.

I had just graduated from college and had my first job on the town newspaper. I dated a guy for about four months who turned out to be abusive. After the first slap, I was done. I broke it off with him and it took me a long time before I even wanted to look at guys. That all changed when I started to attend a new church and there he was.
 He greeted me at the door that first day with a huge smile on his face. I never got past that smile. He had a job on the police force and was four years older than me. It seemed like I had all that I could want. We had three wonderful years together, great years.
 We laughed, skied, went to concerts, went to church together and had so much fun. He finished my sentences and I his.

We would laugh and laugh. I never thought I could be so happy. We were talking about marriage and buying a home. I found someone I could finally be me with.

I had starting writing the second year we were together, while working at the newspaper. I got published that year and did we celebrate! He was so proud of me. I quit my newspaper job and I hired a young college girl to help me out with my books.
 Emily ran all my errands and proofread my manuscripts. We became very close. And then life as I knew it ended.
 It ended because Emily also had an abusive boyfriend. Maybe that's why I understood her so well. She confided in me and I tried to help her. Adam was controlling and angry and had a gun.

One Friday night she called frantic after locking herself in the bathroom. We immediately went to their apartment. He had been drinking and had broken in the bathroom door, yelling at her and waving the gun. Caleb tried to get between Adam and Emily, trying to calm him down. He died trying to protect her. Adam shot them both. He ran out the door after the shooting and was arrested at his parent's house a few hours later.

Emily died on the bathroom floor that day, and Caleb died on the way to the hospital. My life felt like it ended that day. The funeral was a blur. I just shut down. I didn't want to do anything. I quit going to church, I quit talking to God. Where was HE in this? Why did HE take him? Why Emily? Why did HE spare me?? My mom continued to tell me "Sarah, God hasn't left you. He is carrying you right now honey. You can do ALL things through Christ who strengthens you." I didn't want to hear it. I was mad at God!
 My mom would look at me and very quietly say "Sarah, I hope you dance." which in mom terms means get on with my life and be happy. I'm trying to mom.

Hannah came every day and sat with me and held me while I cried. Raeghen flew out from New York and consoled me. Getting through the trial was horrible.

I had to testify, as I was the eyewitness. They gave him life in prison. Raeghen and Hannah were both there through this senseless tragedy, the funeral, the trial, and both with me now, pushing me, wanting the best. If you have one good friend through life that is wonderful, but two and it's amazing. I have two.

I realized Maggie and I ended up in front of our house. I unlocked the door and turned at the sound of a tan truck driving by slowly, the same tan truck that was in the garage from the red house. The same guy standing in the garage from the red house was driving by. I hurried and unlocked the door and pushed Maggie in. Involvement I didn't want, nor did I was to be labeled as a nosy new neighbor.

Chapter 2

I went back to my unpacking, and Maggie went back to chasing birds and squirrels in the yard. The rest of the day went surprisingly fast. After eating a light dinner, I went to bed early. Maggie lay on the end of the bed as usual. My protector.

Tomorrow would be a new day and the town was a few miles away, which I would be investigating. I needed a new printer cartridge and more paper. I had to remember to ask Mrs. Lane about that house next to me. Sleep didn't come easy. It never did. I would sleep a few hours, and lay awake thinking, thinking. It seemed normal anymore, the lack of sleeping.

I woke in the morning ready for a new day. I put on the coffee as I read the mail from yesterday. I had all my mail forwarded from Montana so I was a few days late in reading it. Hannah sent me pictures of our friends from church. There were a group of us, both singles and couples that got together for just about everything. We had a lot of fun. Hannah was always the life of the party, but when Caleb died I didn't feel I belonged with the group. Not that they didn't try. It just brought back too many painful memories, so I pretty much stayed home.

It was hard being alone after being with someone. Alone to eat, alone to shop, alone at night watching TV. I was finding it was a big adjustment, but it was good to see them all laughing in the pictures. I really did miss them.

There were a few advertisements, a magazine and a cell phone bill. I dropped them on the desk for later and grabbed my bag, Maggie and my keys. I locked the house and we were off
. After backing my Jeep out of the driveway we drove out of the neighborhood onto the main road

. We were only about seven or eight miles from the main town of St. Joseph, which according to Sam my realtor had about 8,400 people.

As we drove I found the office supply store near the center of town. I got two ink cartridges and a couple reams of paper. It was morning and still cool outside so locking Mags in the Jeep with the windows rolled down a bit would be OK. First I walked back to the bluff that overlooked the pier. The sight was wonderful. There was a carousel down on the beach. I watched that merry-go- round for quite a while before I wandered down the block window- shopping.

I found a quaint little restaurant called Tony's. Breakfast sounded good and besides I would be expanding my horizons since I never ate alone. But this seemed OK, small, not a lot of people and mostly booths. I found one near the back and sat down and began to look around. I loved this place! It was like you took a step back into the fifties. A lot of Motown music was playing, even this early, and I loved Motown. I looked up and there was an actual little train that ran completely around the top of the room. It was built on a shelf that hung a couple of feet down from the ceiling. There were lights strung around the track. It was so unique and I loved watching that train go round.

Two older couples sat a table in the middle of the room laughing and eating. A woman with two small children was in another booth. The kids were also fascinated with the train. Then I looked sideways and there staring back at me was the guy from the red house in the woods. He gave me a pleasant nod and went back to reading his paper.

I felt myself blush and looked at the menu. Wonder if he recognized me as the nut that stood in the center of the road staring? Oh I hope not.

"Are you ready to order?" a voice asked. I looked up. A guy around fifty or so stood there with an apron on so I gathered maybe he was the waiter? "Sure I'll have the pancakes and a cup of coffee." I said with a slight smile.

"The Blueberry pancakes are the best, my specialty, no extra charge." he said. "OK, then I'll try those." I replied. He brought back a steaming cup of strong coffee and left. O K, I can do this. Quiet place, not a lot of people, and Mags would lie down in the car and wait patiently. I put some sugar in my coffee and casually glance around as I stirred it.

The guy from the red house got up and went and paid his bill. He joked with the waiter as if they knew each other and then left without another glance. Good maybe he didn't recognize me. My pancakes came a few minutes later. Three large ones covering the entire plate and more fresh coffee. They were delicious under thick, dark maple syrup. The blueberries were so big and oozing with flavor.

The waiter rang up my bill and introduced himself as Tony. He said he owned the cafe with his wife Gabby. He asked me if I was new in town or just a tourist. I replied the first hoping he didn't want a lot of information too. He didn't. "I know how hard it is if you don't know a lot of people. Gabby ran our granddaughters to dance, but I'm sure she'd love to meet you. Stop by again." "Thanks, I will." I replied as I paid my bill. He gave me a friendly "Bye than" as I left.

This town may not be too bad a place to start over I thought. Mags was ready to go when I got back to the jeep. She had waited patiently and now wanted out.

We drove back to the quiet neighborhood and I parked my jeep. I decided Raeghen had waited long enough and I wanted to get going on my book again.

After some work maybe Maggie and I would take a run on the beach. Maybe go by that house next door and get a better look. Mags took out the back door of the porch and played in the yard chasing squirrels or whatever she was chasing.

I took my laptop on the back porch and sat at the table with another cup of coffee and began to write.
I put a dragon fly on the page, my trademark, and started writing. It felt good to put words on paper again. I was in to a series of books and Carly; my heroine was solving another murder and looking quite good while she did it. If only real life was that way.

I was always self-conscious of my looks. I felt I was too tall at five feet eight. I had long dark thick hair, which had a mind of its own. Everyone told me I could stand to put on a few pounds but when life hits you smack in the face; you don't feel like eating. Well maybe I'm getting my appetite back if breakfast was any indication. I'd have to stop back there and try lunch one day, maybe invite Mrs. Lane if she was up to it.

OK, back to the job of writing. Actually it never felt like a job. Mom always said I had a vivid imagination when I was young and evidently it carried over. I never knew the end of my stories. I just wrote it as it came. I loved it.

After several hours I got up and stretched. It was starting to get warm out so I changed into some shorts. Looking out I saw Mags lying under one of the trees dozing. Maybe a run and a little exploring. I got my house keys and gave her a call as I went out the backdoor.

Great, a little soft breeze was starting to blow, cooling off this heat. We walked down to the small gate that opened onto the beach. Unlocking it I pushed it open and Maggie went rushing out to the water. I swear she is ninety-five percent water dog!
She dived into the cool waves and barked at each one that came her way. I started laughing and jogging to the left, down the beach looking up as I went by the big-gated house.

There was a patio on the back overlooking an overgrown back yard that led down to the beach. Someone was sitting at a table and chairs on that patio.

They practically flew into the house as I looked up. I stopped dead in my tracks with Maggie running into me.   Odd behavior I thought. Why the frantic hurry to get into the house? I stood there for a minute just looking at the house.

Maybe it's the mystery writer in me but now I was just downright curious. I stood there and watched to see if I could see anything else. Nothing. Wait, one of the curtains was drawn back but I couldn't see anyone. You know that feeling, when the hairs on the back of your neck stand up?
You can't put your finger on it but something is wrong. Way wrong. That is the way I felt looking at that house.

Well now's the time to get a move on. "Come on Mags." and I began to jog again down the beach. I ran at an even pace with the slight breeze in my face. The mist from the waves felt good in this heat
. Ahead of me there was someone standing by a boat dock on the shore. As I got closer there as the guy from the red house. How could I stop suddenly, turn around and go back without seeming like, well, a complete dork! So I kept running. He looked up and stared at me as I approached. I slowed down and jogged slowly by with a "Hi there." and a slight smile. He seemed sort of amused and smiled. What was
that? I mean couldn't he at least say hi? Did he think, oh no, he knew it was me! The idiot that stood in the street staring, now I really felt dumb. Oh brother, did he think I was stalking him? First his house, then Tony's and now here at his house again.

Now if this were one of my books, I would have some way out of this embarrassing situation. Maybe some boat would pull up on the water and I could just hop on and off we'd go. Or a helicopter.

Ah that could be sort of cool, a helicopter would hover down out of the sky, I would grab a rope and they'd pull me up, whoever they are, and I would be looking oh so good while I did it. Wait. I could dream up stories even on a run! Get hold of yourself, he is JUST a guy on the beach and I have no interest whatsoever of meeting him. Boy I do need to get a grip and get back to the books!

With a call to Mags we turned around and back we headed. He was on his cell phone when I went back by, thank goodness, and we ran past and back down the beach to our gate.

We went in and up the back yard to the porch. I unlocked the back door and went in to the ringing of my own cell. It was Sam, my realtor, wanting to make sure all was OK with the house. Assuring him it was, I thanked him again for helping with the movers and for calling.

Chapter 3

After we hung up I gave Mags some fresh water in her bowl and went back out on to the porch to write some more. I did get another three chapters in before calling it quits. It was getting late, near dinnertime.

I decided to try out my new BBQ grill. It was a small one on a stand. I really didn't need anything big and I had purchased it right before the move. In fact, I purchased all my furniture before moving and packed all that I had in boxes.

It was all here waiting for me when I got here thanks to Sam who let them in to unload. He did a pretty good job with arranging the living room furniture. I left it how he had arranged it when I came. I liked it. The couch was so comfortable I was glad I picked it. Wasn't too sure about the light color but with the new throw pillows it was just right. They were the color of fall. I love those colors. They seem warm and inviting.

I was just taking the steaks out of the fridge, one for me and one for Mags when there was a knock on the back screen door. I sort of jumped after that odd feeling I had down on the beach and looked around the corner to see Red House Guy standing there. He had a six-pack of Coke and a smile on his face. "Hope I'm not interrupting?" he said through the screen raising the coke for me to see.

"No, not at all." I said coming to the back door with the package still in my hands. "Well I thought I'd better do the neighborly thing and come introduce myself. I'm Connor." "Well, it's nice to meet you, I'm Sarah." I just stood there and stared at him.
 What did the cat have my tongue? No, the cat evidently tied up my tongue because I couldn't really say anything, just look.

He was beautiful to look at! What was he doing here? Again that amused smile. "Were you taking that package somewhere?" he asked nodding towards my hands. "Oh, oh no…I mean yes…no it's steaks, we were going to grill."

He looked around for the "we". "No, Maggie and I" I replied to his silent question and nodded to Maggie who now considered this man her best friend evidently, tail wagging and snuggling up to him. Traitor. He leaned down and petted her, and rubbed her behind the ears. Always the ears. How do these people know her tender spot? How come she didn't bark when he walked up to the door? That was interesting.

"Oh sorry to interrupt your dinner. I can come back later." he said. "You're welcome to stay…just steaks and a salad, nothing fancy." I said wondering why in the world would I invite a perfect stranger to dinner. For all I knew this could turn out horrible. Why he could be ax murderer or a serial killer! And Maggie would not be pleased having to give up her steak.

"Sure!" he said with a smile. So he did the grilling and I made a salad. Not a bad team, wait that twinge of sadness and guilt crept in again. Sometimes I felt I shouldn't be having fun, that maybe somehow, even though I knew better, that I was betraying Caleb. But it had been a year as Raeghen said and this was NOT a date…just meeting a neighbor.

In the end, I had a very pleasant evening. We sat and ate the steaks and salad and drank cokes on the back porch and talked and talked. I kept wondering to myself as to why I was so comfortable. I liked that feeling again.

He lived in his house for the past eight months. He lived in town before that but wanted to move by the beach. He said he was a consultant at the power plant here. I told him a little about me, how I moved here from Montana. "To get out of the cold." I said. Caleb was my story and I didn't want to share him just now. Sitting there listening to the waves and watching lightning bugs was so relaxing.

Talking about St. Joe, the weather and the neighborhood. "Hey," I said, "What do you know about that house next to me?" I asked pointing to it.

"I really don't know anything why?" he asked. I told him the strange feeling I had, how the person, man or woman, I didn't know which, ran back into the house when they saw me.
How the curtains were pulled back but I couldn't see anyone. "It's probably nothing." he said. He didn't seem real interested.
The evening ended shortly after that. Connor thanked me for the meal and left with an invite for a boat ride. He headed out the back door of the porch and down the yard to the gate on the beach. A quick wave and he was gone. Boy he seemed in a hurry.

"Not too bad of an evening." I said to Maggie as I cleared the plates. She totally ignored me. The only thing that was on her mind was those steak bones, which she thoroughly enjoyed when I gave them to her. Locking up, I headed for bed.

Chapter 4

Now, in the dark, with Maggie growling, thinking back on all of those events, my mind raced. My eyes were still adjusting to the dark watching Maggie get off the bed still growling and creeping slowly to the bedroom door. I got up and pulled on my sweat bottoms. My heart was starting to pound. I looked around the room, no weapon and no gun. Caleb had wanted me to get a gun for protection in Montana but I refused. I had taken some boxing and karate lessons instead. I told him I could defend myself. Now I doubted that. I had told Caleb God would watch out for me. But now, God and I weren't exactly on speaking terms.

I slowly opened the bedroom door and she walked slowly out into the living room and then suddenly stormed the back door barking wildly! My heart was now beating so loudly in my ears I realized I was holding my breath. I felt like I was frozen in my spot. I made myself walk over to the wall and switch on all the outside lights. Sam told me there were floodlights in the backyard put in by the previous owner and he wasn't kidding. The whole back yard lit up all the way down to the beach. They could probably see me from space with all those lights, and how I was grateful! I knew the screen door on the porch was locked, so I grabbed a rolling pin out of the crock on the floor and opened the back door, no one was there. Maggie went out onto the big screened porch...and then I saw it. The screen on the door had been slit. I didn't go out, too nervous by this point.

My porch door was locked; I did that when Connor left. I always locked the screen door, the porch door and then the inside door.

Caleb told me by locking the screen door it's just one more obstacle the intruder would have to go through giving you more time to call 911. It became a habit, which now I was glad of. Being a cop he was always giving me little safety tips

. But now, looking at the screen, somebody tried to get in. Why? Maggie was still barking but calmer now. Evidently whoever was outside had taken off when the lights came on or they heard Maggie. That's a relief I thought but realized I was pretty shaken up. I left those lights on all night and slept on the couch with Maggie staring intently at the back door. I must have fallen asleep because my cell phone was ringing in my ear.

"Hello?" "Sarah! I've been calling and calling! Where are you?" Hannah said in the phone. "Oh I'm so sorry; I must have slept through it. I had a little excitement in the night. Maggie heard something." then I explained the events that followed.

"Oh my gosh Sarah, are you OK? You sure you don't just want to come back home?" Hannah asked with alarm in her voice. "No, no, really I'm fine. We're all good here. When are you coming?" I asked. "Well that's why I'm calling. Hopefully next month I can get away. I'm just breaking in a new girl and Heda had some knee surgery so I have to wait till she gets back."

Hannah owned a small vintage boutique and Heda had been with her for years. She did quite well in the store selling beautiful vintage clothing and wonderful hats! How we loved those hats! And Hannah loved Heda even more, who turned out to be more like a mother to her than an employee. Her own mother died when Hannah was young and she grew a strong attachment to Heda who felt the same, so I knew she wouldn't leave until she was sure Heda felt better.

"No hurry, take your time. I will be ready to show you some sights because by then I will know where they all are!" I told her. We talked a few minutes more and said good-bye.

I got up off the couch and let Maggie out the back doors. I went out and looked around. Nothing. I could hear the waves but nothing seemed amiss, except for the slit in the screen. It was odd.

Why? Who? After making coffee I jumped in for a quick shower and got dressed. When I got out I could hear talking. I stopped dead in my tracks. Then I heard Maggie. She sounded excited.

I walked to the back door and there stood Connor petting her and rubbing her ears. The ears again. He looked up and "Hey is everything OK here?" Instantly I wondered why.
Why would he ask me that? Did he know something? Was it him who was creeping around in the night slitting my screen? No it couldn't have been, he was so nice. Get a grip girl.

"Why?" I asked. "Sarah, your floodlights are bright enough to light up a stadium. I saw them on in the middle of the night when I went to get a glass of water. They lit up half the beach, and your screen is cut!" "No, all is OK I guess. Mags just heard something in the middle of the night and after I saw the screen I didn't want to turn them off." I said.

"Well I can look around and make sure everything else is OK and then we call the police. I'm also gona leave you my cell number. If that happens again you call me, you hear? I'm only a couple houses down. I can run down the beach and be here in a second. You sure you're OK?" There was no mistaken the concern in his voice.

"Yes were fine. Really." I said not so sure but trying to convince myself as well as him. He called the police on his cell and within a few minutes an officer was there. I led him through the house to the screen door. "Not much we can do but start patrolling a little more on your street. I'll tell the second and third shift officers to keep a lookout and it wouldn't hurt to keep that back light on for a while." he said with an encouraging smile. "Don't hesitate to call 911 you hear?" he said. I nodded and Connor walked him out.

I was still a little shaken when Connor came back and handed me a small piece of paper with his number on it and said "Now put that in your phone and make it a speed dial so you just have to hit one number. It's faster that way. I charge my phone on my nightstand so I'll hear it.

I'm a light sleeper anyway and make sure you lock your doors tonight." Seriously, no seriously, I thought, did he just tell me that? What woman living alone leaves her doors unlocked??

"OK, thanks but really we're fine." I wasn't as sure as I said it and I think he caught the edge in my voice. "I'll give Jim a call down at the lumber yard and see about replacing that screen. No sense in taking chances." he said as turned to walk around.
A few minutes later after assuring me all was OK in the back yard he got ready to leave. "Call me, I mean it, and I'll let you know when they will be here to fix the door." he said and left.

We watched him walk through the gate and down the beach. Well that was sort of nice I thought. A neighbor with concern. Then Maggie started barking again! There was knocking on my front door. Boy this sure didn't turn out to be the quiet getaway I hoped for. I opened it to find a middle-aged pudgy couple standing there with big grins on their face.

"Hi" the man said. The lady, who I assumed was his wife, was grinning also. She was heavyset with bleached blond hair that was not becoming at all and had on too much makeup. He was short and had one of those ridiculous toupees on. It was horrible and I kept staring at it. It's like driving by a car accident. It's so horrible and you shouldn't look but you can't take your eyes off of it! He had big thick black glasses and was sort of seedy looking. I was not at all comfortable with those two on my front steps. "Hello. Can I help you?" I asked staring at his head. "We're your neighbors over here he pointed a stubby finger to a white house on the other side of mine.

"I'm Frank Bellows and this is Marjorie, my wife." They seemed familiar but I just couldn't place them. Get a grip and quit staring at his head! Maybe I had seen them in a store or at Tony's.

"Oh, I'm Sarah" I just stared at them. "Can we come in and visit? We just moved in a week or so ago." he said rather rudely I thought. "I'm sorry, I was just leaving" I lied. Maggie had not stopped barking for which I was glad of. I was blocking the door with my body so she wouldn't go through. He looked at the door seeming a little afraid and stepped back.

"So you have a dog?" "Yup" I replied. "She is rather protective and doesn't warm up to strangers." not knowing why I said that. "Maybe we could visit another time, but right now I'm late for an appointment." another lie. I'm gona have to have Mrs. Lane pray for me. She did say she went to church and right now my church life was in the toilet. I could use all the help in that area I could get.

They stepped back and turned to leave with a little irritation on their face? I couldn't be sure. "Sure, sure, we'll come back another time." he said with shortness in his voice and off they stomped.
 "I hope a big wind doesn't come Mags, he'll lose his hair, but then really, that would be a blessing in disguise. I guess this is not the quiet place we thought it was. All this excitement and noisiness!" She growled in reply as they walked down the walk. Were they the ones stalking around in the middle of the night? Mags sure didn't like them and neither did I.

Chapter 5

Well since I lied and told them we were leaving, I thought I better at least take a ride or risk the chance of them coming back. Better yet, now would be a time to go seek out a security system for my house. I'd seen them advertised on TV and I was sure there was one in town. I grabbed the local phone book and leafed through the pages till I found two names and numbers of companies who installed the systems. I locked up and Maggie and I headed into town.

After trying the first name on the list and finding their office locked up with the lights off, I headed down the street to the second name. I'm glad I did. The girl at the desk was so helpful, showed me the prices and dates they could come out and install the system. Everything seemed so reasonable, so I made an appointment for the next afternoon at two. After paying for the system I left feeling a little bit safer even if
I had to go one more night without it. I decided I would stop in again at Tony's for a quick cup of coffee before heading home. After giving her a quick potty walk, Mags hopped up into the jeep for a nap. I headed to Tony's.

I walked in the door and was greeted to my surprise, like an old friend. "Sarah!" he yelled from the back. I was a little bit embarrassed but it felt good that he remembered me. "Hi Tony" I smiled. "Have a seat Sarah, Gabby will be right out. She can't wait to meet you." he said. Sure enough here came Gabby, Tony's wife. I instantly liked her. She had a big smile on her face and came right over. "Hi Sarah, I'm Gabby. Tony told me you came in and I've been waiting to meet you. How do you like St. Joe?"

"Well, actually I like it a lot. I bought a cottage on the beach and it's so relaxing. I'm glad I came." she looked genuinely interested and asked if she could sit down. I nodded and she said "First, let me get us something to sip on, coffee? Tea? Malt?"

Ah, the yummy fattening cool milkshake. She saw my eyes and said "Give me a sec and I'll go make us a couple, on the house." and off she went. Well this is certainly my kind of girl I thought. She was back in a few minutes with two tall glasses of thick, chocolate malt. We sipped on them and just chatted back and forth like old girlfriends. She was not prying either. She told me how Tony and her were high school sweethearts. After graduation Tony went to navy and she went to college. When he got out they got married and bought this little cafe. "Been here ever since. Raised our two kids, they both worked here, and now I get to have my grandkids around."

"Are you single? If I'm not prying? Tony said he didn't know if you had family here?" "Well, "I started, "I have a distant uncle in Indiana but no, I don't have any close family here. Just me and Maggie my dog." "Hon," she said, "don't rush anything. Life is so full of surprises and I am finding out that Father God has quite a sense of humor sometimes. Life is a trip!" she laughed.

So she was in touch with God too. Boy, everyone I meet lately is in touch with HIM but me. I really like this woman I thought as I sat sipping my malt. I told her what happened in the night and with the screen door. "Sarah, don't take any chances!" she said with concern. I told her about the security system and she looked relieved.

We visited a few minutes longer, both slurped our malts and I got ready to leave. "Thanks so much for the malt Gabby, it was really so nice to meet you!"
"You too, Sarah, don't be a stranger. Make sure you stop and let us know you're OK." She gave me a friendly hug. I waved to Tony and out the door I went.

I really like this place I thought, well, except for the slit screen door, and well, the nosy neighbors next door, and well, that odd house. Stop it; this is not one of your books. These people are probably all right. Am I trying to convince myself?

Probably a bunch of kids trying to have a party on the beach or something. The something was what I was nervous about.

We headed home and pulled into the driveway. I looked over to see Frank and Marjorie out in their front yard fiddling with their flowers. Are they watching me? I thought. Odd. I nodded to them hoping they wouldn't come over, and went in the house. Maybe I'm just jittery. Now I'm thinking the neighbors are watching me!

I still had the better part of the day and if I wanted to get a run in, I'd better get some work done. So taking my laptop out to the porch again, I began to write. I was totally engrossed in my story. I stopped for a quick salad around one and then started writing again. I loved my book; I always did when I wrote.

Carly, my heroine always got into predicaments. She always came out of it looking well. Of course you can make life just how you want it in a book. You can escape into a world of mystery, loved, death, and always come out well. Not so in life I found out.

After writing for most of the day, I had a light supper, and nestled into my couch with a bowl of hot buttery popcorn, my downfall. Popcorn was comfort food to me and even Maggie liked it. I kept the back porch light on like the police suggested.

We watched a movie, locked the doors and headed to the bedroom. After I got in bed, with Mags on the end of it, I lay there thinking. For the most part I felt I was doing OK. If I just kept busy I didn't think too much. Just wasn't sure what I was going to do with my life. Hope didn't seem to be at the end of my tunnel. I knew in my heart God was still there, I wasn't. I didn't want to forgive HIM quite yet.

I finally drifted off to sleep and slept a couple of hours till I got up for a glass of water. I was still a little nervous as I went into the kitchen, which faced the big brick house next to me.

Even with the large lot separating the houses I could see there was a light on in the upstairs window. I looked at the clock on the kitchen wall. The moonlight shined on it. Three AM.

Wonder what that's all about? Wonder if it was a he or she that ran in the house that day I was running by. Oh well, better get back to bed and try for more sleep. I looked down and there stood Mags looking up. "Come on girl, and thanks for the company. I'm actually glad you're so protective."

We walked into the bedroom and got back in bed and I heard her sigh as she got situated at the end of the bed. I was thankful for her. Sleep finally came and I woke up to the phone again.

Chapter 6

"Hello?" "Sarah?" This is Melanie from Safe Systems. I just wanted to confirm your appointment with the technician for installing your security system today at two." "Oh yes, I'll be here." I replied sitting up. I looked over at the clock. Ten fifteen! Had I really slept that late? I can't remember when I did that before; usually I'm up at the crack of dawn.

"OK, Mark Hanson will be there right around two to install. He will have identification too." she said. "That's great Melanie, thanks so much." I said. With that we hung up and I got up and let Mags out.
I made some coffee and then took a long shower, more to wake me up. I hadn't been sleeping very well lately, that's probably why I slept so late, I thought, it finally caught up with me. Caleb use to tell me not to worry so much about sleeping, that eventually it would catch up. That never seemed to work for me. Maybe now it was, I thought as I got dressed.

I cleaned up the living room and had a cup of coffee. I walked out on the screened porch and sat in my porch swing to watch the waves and drink coffee. This really was a great location; and relaxing too. I was thankful I didn't have to get up and rush to work every morning. I was fortunate to do something I loved, and from home. Maggie was chasing something around the tree in the back yard and barking. She liked it here also. That was a good sign.

I caught movement out of my eye to the left. The house next door, someone was outside. I stood up seeing if I could notice anything. Nothing. Wait, someone was out on that patio. I couldn't see as there were some trees between the houses. Maybe I should be the neighbor to walk over and say hi. Maybe I would.

I grabbed Maggie's leash and locked the house and started down the front walk to the street. I got to the black iron fence. The tall gate had a latch with a padlock on it from the inside.
That's strange, I thought. Maybe they don't want to be disturbed, maybe recluses. Well, that wouldn't stop the mystery writer in me. I'll just go around back!

So back to my house I went, and through the yard down to my gate. We went out on the beach and I walked to the back of the mystery house. I didn't have to go up those long stairs to the patio because she was coming down the stairs! Wow, I was just in time.

She was in her thirties, I'd say, tall, long wild looking curly red hair and very thin. She was extremely haggard looking. She just stopped wide- eyed and stared at me. I don't think she even saw me as she walked down the stairs. I was right in front of her.

"Hello." I said hoping to engage her in conversation. "I'm Sarah, I live right next door." I said pointing back to my house. She looked very surprised. "I really don't have time right now." she said abruptly and turned around and went back up the stairs.

"Wow" I said to Mags who was more interested in trying to get in the water. I was shocked. What the heck? Now I was even more curious. I continued down the beach. No one else seemed to be out enjoying this weather. What? Was I looking for Connor? No way! Get your head on girl! You do NOT need any involvement. So we turned around and headed back to our house. I looked up as we walked by the brick house and could see no one. Very odd.

As I was walking up the stairs to my backyard, I saw Connor at the top. He must have come around from the front.
"Hey Sarah, Tom is here from the lumber yard fixing your screen." he said as he nodded to an older looking man just finishing the repair job. I went in and got him a check and paid him.

I better do the same as I had some time to get back to my book before the security company came. I took my laptop back out to the back porch. I was going to have to use my office when the weather turned, but now I really enjoyed sitting on the porch, listening to the waves and writing.

Today, I had trouble getting into it as I was more curious about the redhead next door. What was her story? Why so rude? Wash she some kind of recluse? Heck I guess I was trying to be a bit of a recluse too. It's just that I knew my story and I didn't know hers.

I tried to work but found I couldn't concentrate so I closed my laptop and went back into the living room. I looked around and decided maybe I could tackle a few more boxes. There were only about six boxes left. The ones I didn't want to deal with, those with pictures of Caleb and our life together, I stacked in the living room closet for later. I just didn't want to feel bad right now. I got through about three boxes before I decided to have lunch. Today just a salad and then back to business.

The phone range twice, once from Sam making sure all was OK, and the other was Mark, from Security Systems telling me he'd be coming right around two.

I kept thinking about the red haired lady next door. I couldn't imagine what her story was but my mind was exploring every possibility. Maybe I could write her into my book. There was a knock on the door.

I looked at the clock, one fifteen. Mark was early. I opened the door to find Mrs. Lane. "Mrs. Lane!" I was excited to see her. "Do come in, I'm so happy you came! I said almost out of breath. I was really excited to see her. "Oh dear, I have Monty and Tilly with me, maybe I should just stay out here and we could talk on the porch." she said to a chorus of pug snorting.

"Nonsense! Come in. Bring them. They are welcome and can go out with Mags in the back yard. Don't worry it's fenced all the way down to the beach so they will be safe." I said.

"OK, then come on boys and girls" she said as they did the pug snorting again and came waddling in very excited to see me with more snorting and kisses. Mags heard them and was racing around the couch with them in hot pursuit. I t was so funny watching them run round and round.

"OK guys, come on outside, you have a whole yard with lots of trees to chase in" as I opened the porch door and then the outside door. I told her about the cut in the screen. "Sarah, what happened?" she asked with alarm. I told her about the night and Connor showing up as we watched the three dogs racing outside barking at each other and playing.

She was very concerned about my safety. We were laughing as we watched the dogs. "But let me show you the house Mrs. Lane; but don't mind it, not everything is in order yet" I said.

"Oh Sarah, it's so nice and comfortable. I love the soft fall colors you picked. Your couch looks so comfortable" she said as she surveyed the living room. I took her on a small tour. I was very pleased she liked it. I felt so comfortable around her.

We went back to the screened porch and sat down. "I hope we're not interrupting, we decided to take a little walk and I just wanted to see how you were doing. I also wanted to talk to you about something. I'm not stopping you from writing am I?" she asked. "Oh no, today was a slow day so I decided to unpack some of the last boxes and I was waiting for the security man to come. I'm having a security system put in." I told her.

"Oh yes, that would be a very smart thing to do with that screen and all" she said. "We put one in several years ago and I'm glad we did. You are hooked up directly to a center where if there are any problems they will call 911 or the police directly."

"That's what I thought." I replied. "Well you have made the right decision Sarah. The boys and girls always let me know if someone is around but I don't think they would be much protection." she said smiling. I suddenly had that pictured in my mind.
 Burglar comes in and trips, Monty waddles over, bites the top of his shoe and climbs on top of him doing the pug snorting and kisses and Tilly barking up a storm…too funny.

 I came back to reality when I heard her say, "Sometimes I think your new neighbors near the A Frames are skulking around." I burst out laughing.

"Oh Mrs. Lane, I haven't heard that word for ages. My dad would to say that. But what do you mean? Because to tell you the truth they came over here but I didn't let them in…. just something wrong about them." I said.

"Well when I'm out front in my flowers I see them staring at your house. Not too sure about those two Sarah and have you seen his hair? "she said. I immediately started laughing and we had a big discussion about the "rug" on his head.

"The real reason I came over" she said, "was to see what you thought about a neighborhood party. We use to have them a lot when Todd was still alive. Everyone would bring a dish and we'd cook hamburgers and hotdogs and just relax and connect. It would give you a chance to meet everyone. There are about six families I would invite plus the new neighbors of course, if you don't think that will be too many. Some probably won't come. Children too, would that be OK?" she asked.
 She continued before I answered "But if you think you are not ready for that we can always think about it another time." she said as she looked at me with a smile. I loved this woman. I just felt she maybe sensed something.

I surprised even myself when I said "No I think that's a great idea. We can have it here. I certainly have the room for it. If the weather changes, we can come into the back porch. The yard is quite large and goes all the way down to the beach. I think it's a great idea. But I'm not sure about my other neighbor in the brick house. I tried to introduce myself but she wanted no part of it. I would also have to get a larger grill as mine is pretty small."

"Well as far as the grill goes, I know Connor has a large one and I know he would be willing to bring it. Maybe we can even get him to do the grilling. Men like to grill you know. What do you think of him dear?" she asked.

"He seems very nice." Was I blushing? Oh my gosh get a grip! "He came over and introduced himself, seemed real nice." She smiled.

"He is Sarah. He would help you in a minute should you need anything. We will get him to help. I will invite everyone. How does Saturday around four or five sound? That would give us a couple of days to get everything ready and to ask everyone. If that doesn't work for you, we can wait a week or so. What do you think?" she asked.

"That sounds great! I'll make a bunch of snacks and dips and we will have a great time. And where would you suggest we get the meat? I'm not real familiar with the stores, although I have seen a van from Whole Foods come next door to the brick house. I don't think she goes out much."

"Let me take care of the meat Sarah. My brother owns the Butcher Block in St. Joe. He is always giving me all kinds of meat. Trust me, it will cost very little. You grab some hamburger and hot dog buns and I will grab the meat. Deal?" she asked. "Great!" I replied to some knocking on the front door. I hadn't realized the time went by so quickly. "That must be Mark form Safe Security." I went to let him in.

He was in his late forties I'd say, very nice and immediately introduced himself and showed me his ID. As he entered he looked across the room. "Hey Mrs. Lane how are you today?" he asked my new friend.

Ah good he knew her. "Mark how nice to see you. How are Diane and the kids?" Evidently they knew each other well. "Sarah, Mark and I go to church together. You are in good hands here."
Church, hmm, are You trying to tell me something God? I'm still upset with You. "Well good. Do you need me to do anything? Move anything for you?" I asked him. "No, all good, it should take me about two hours and I will teach you how to use it. The system is very simple but very safe." he said.

Mrs. Lane left after a few goodbyes and a promise to see Mark in church on Sunday. We had a little trouble getting the "boys and girls" as she called Monty and Tilly away from Maggie. Boy had they become fast friends. I decided to go back out on the porch and try to write a few more chapters.
It also gave me time to contemplate my red haired neighbor. I was not sure what was going on with her but I was determined to find out.

Mark was right about the two hours. In no time he was done and showing me the control box. He explained everything very simply and left a manual, which was, believe it or not, not four inches thick and in a foreign language! It seemed simple to read and had pictures. That right there was worth its weight in gold. He also left me his cell number in case I had trouble setting it. Wow, you never find that in the city. He left shortly after that with an invitation, if I was looking, to try out the church that Mrs. Lane and his family attended. No pressure he said. The church would love to have me. I thanked him and told him I would think about it.

I waved as I watched him back his van out of the driveway. I turned to my left. There they were, the Bellows, in their front yard again watching Mark leave. I stepped back glad they saw the truck.

If it were them skulking around as my dad and Mrs. Lane would say, they now know I have a security system that automatically alerts the police.

Chapter 7

I looked up at the clock. Four thirty. There was a knock on the back porch screen door. "Sarah? Are you home?" Connor yelled through the door. "Just a minute, I'm coming" I said. Was I excited? I found myself hurrying to the door. "Hi!" I said excited to see him? No way, I was not going to get involved, at least he wasn't a policeman or FBI. No way was I ever going to get involved with law enforcement again. Too big a chance of getting hurt.

"Mrs. Lane gave me a call and told me about the big cookout. Thought I'd come down and get our plans on the same page." he said with a smile. "Sure come on in." I said as Maggie attached him with kisses and wiggling. "OK Mags, what? Do I have a treat? Why yes I do!" he said as he pulled out a dog bone out of his pocket. She grabbed the bone and off she went. "You spoil her." I said.

He followed me to the kitchen table where I had the papers about the security system on the table. "Sarah this is good! You got a system installed?" he asked. "I did, in fact this afternoon. Mark just left. It seems simple enough. He showed me how to set it when I leave and disarm it when I come in. I feel a lot better now." I said. "Good" he said firmly with a nod.

I grabbed a couple of pops out of the fridge and sat down. We discussed what we would need and the time he would bring down his grill. He offered to bring some extra chairs and volleyball net and croquet for the kids. Did people still play croquet? Evidently, as he was bringing it.

I thought that was thoughtful for the kids. He offered to bring a cooker to do a shrimp boil along with corn on the cob. All this food talk was making me hungry.

"Wow Sarah it's already six. You want to go into Tony's and get something to eat?" he asked. "Sure, I'm starving" I replied. We got Maggie and he helped me set the alarm system and we went out the front door.

"Let's take my jeep." I said and handed him the keys. I put Maggie in the back seat where she immediately laid down and got cozy on her blanket. I jumped in the passenger seat thinking how nice it was to have someone else drive.

The night was warm and we rolled the windows down. We talked about the BBQ some more as we drove into town and parked in front of Tony's. The streets were crowded with tourists. It was fun seeing all the people going in and out of the shops. I spied an ice cream parlor I hadn't seen before as we walked into Tony's.

"Connor, Sarah!" came a voice from the back. Tony came out smiling as patrons looked up from their meals. "Come on back here." he said and pointed to a cozy booth. "Sarah!" I heard Gabby and turned around to see her smiling face. She came up and gave me a hug as well as Connor.

"Hey Gabs" he said returning the smile. "Are you keeping her safe Connor? She had some trouble the other night." "Yes, I am so don't worry." Connor replied. After a little more small talk we sat down and ordered a couple of hamburgers and fries. The burgers were huge and so tasty. We had a great dinner with talk of the lake, tourists, Tony and Gabby, all the time avoiding the events at my house. I did feel a little better knowing I had the security system but who was trying to get in and why?

We left a little while later and got Maggie out of the Jeep. We walked down to the ice cream parlor and I waited outside with Mags as he went in and got two cones. We took a long leisurely walk down on the beach while she ran and played in the water and we ate our cones. The night was so warm and a lot of people were out walking on the boardwalk and beach. There was music playing and a soft breeze. I loved it. The stars were all over the sky.

It was beautiful! We headed home shortly after. We never stopped talking. It was a lot of fun.

We pulled into the driveway and I notice the flowerpot on my porch was tipped over and broke. There were flowers strewn everywhere as he headlights lit up the porch as we pulled in. "What the heck" Connor said.
"Stay in the car and lock the door." he said as he got out of the jeep. I was suddenly nervous but I think I was also getting mad. Who knocked over my flowers? Was this an accident? The pot was quite tall and large and would not just fall over without someone physically pushing it over.

He up righted the pot and picked up some large pieces, and then he walked around back. He was gone for a few minutes and then came back. "It's OK, come on let's get you in the house." he said as I unlocked the door and got out. I let Maggie out and she ran around the side to the gate. Connor let her in and she went around back. We unlocked the front door after entering the code in the security system and went in. I knew I was safe when inside so I started flipping on lights.

Connor stood watching me and said nothing. "What?" I said. "Is everything OK with you Sarah? You don't have any problems following you here do you?" he asked. "What do you mean?" I asked.

"Well first the screen and then the flower pot…not a big deal but a little strange." he replied. "Well I just moved here and only know you, Mrs. Lane, Tony and Gabby and the creepy neighbors next door. I can't imagine they would want to harm me in any way." I said.

"Well I don't want you taking any chances. You keep Maggie by you all the time and make sure you don't forget to set this alarm system. Maybe it's all coincidence, but maybe not. No sense in taking chances." he said. "OK?" he asked.

"OK. Thanks so much for dinner, the ice cream and the walk. I loved it all." "Great." he said walking toward the back door. "Let's get Maggie in here and then I'll head home. You have my number on speed dial right?"

"I do thanks." I said as he opened the back door and let Mags in. "It WAS fun wasn't it?" he smiled as he went out the door and down the back to the beach.

I locked up and set the alarm. What WAS going on? Was it a coincidence that the flowerpot was knocked down? It was so large only a hurricane wind would blow it over. Was someone trying to scare me?

I'd think a little more clearly in the morning I thought. I'd have to clean up that mess in the front. I got a glass of ice water and headed into the bedroom as I turned off the lights. I was so thankful to have a dog, especially one as protective as Maggie. I finally fell asleep and slept straight through.

Chapter 8

I woke up around six and took a shower and got dressed. I made a couple pieces of toast and sat at the kitchen table with a cup of coffee and ate. Is it my imagination or was someone trying to get in…or maybe get me out? Was it kids horsing around? Looking out the window I wasn't sure exactly how I felt about the whole thing. I went out to the little shed to see what all was left by the previous owners.

Unlocking the door, I found a small lawn mower, hoses and sure enough another flowerpot. Not quite as large as the one out front but it would do. I found two bags of potting soil and filled the pot half way after lugging it around to the front. I re potted the flowers from the broken pot into the new one. Satisfied it looked OK; I hauled the big pot in pieces to the garbage can by the road. It was already warm outside as I got the broom and was sweeping off the front walk.

"Hi there." I heard a voice and turned around to see my neighbor. She was still in her bathrobe and blonde hair disarrayed. She had a newspaper in her hand. She still had way too much makeup on as she eyed me. "What's with the pot?" she asked. I did not like this woman. No way no how. She and that creepy husband of hers just gave me goose bumps.

"Just changing pots." I said. "The other one got broken." I said as I stared at her. Did they knock it over? I thought. I was very suspicious of them. "Hmmmm" was all she said. Strange! I turned around and kept sweeping feeling her eyes on me. I walked around to the side and locked my gate behind me. Weird!

 I got Maggie and walked into the back porch. It was seven-thirty. Grabbing another cup of coffee, and my laptop I headed to the back porch to write. Thinking about that screen made me mad.

I kept coming back to someone trying to scare me away? I didn't like the feeling. I wrote quite a few pages when I heard Maggie get up. I jerked up to see Connor walking up the stairs from the beach. I watched him and wondered about him. I liked spending time with him but realized I really knew nothing about him. Mrs. Lane hadn't really told me anything about is personal life and he didn't either. Maggie started to wag her tail. He walked up to the screen door and smiled.

"Well I see you two girls made it through the night OK." I smiled as he walked into the back porch and followed me into the kitchen. I glanced at the clock realizing I had been writing an hour. I grabbed another cup and poured him a cup and refilled my own. We sat at the kitchen table and I told him about Mrs. Creepy next door.

"You know Sarah; I'm not really sure what to think. The pot was too heavy to blow over and the screen door was deliberately cut. Not sure who in this neighborhood would do that. Could have been some kids hanging around from the A- Frames, but I wouldn't think so."

"I don't know who it would be Connor or why. Can't say I've made any enemies since I just moved here and I really don't know anyone, almost like someone is trying to run me off? I replied. "I don't know who that would be. Well just don't take any chances." he said. "Don't you have to be to work?" I asked looking up at the clock on the wall. "No, ah I really just consult so I make my own hours."

"Wow that must be nice." I said. "Yea," he smiled, "it is a pretty good job. Well I'll catch up with you later about the BBQ and tie the loose ends up." as he put his cup in the sink. "Sure, that sounds good. I'll call Mrs. Lane this afternoon." "OK, see ya!" he smiled and out the door and down the steps he went.

I tried sitting down with my laptop but no way. My curiosity got the better of me. I grabbed a piece of paper and wrote EVENTS at the top of one column and SUSPECTS at the top of the next column. Now I know I must be losing it…

I'm already trying to find suspects from my neighborhood but there was no getting around strange things were happening and to me.

Slit screen and broken flowerpots went under events. Now who could I suspect? Connor? I would hate to think he might have something to do with it…and never Mrs. Lane.
No it had to be either the two creeps from next door or the redhead from the big house. My bets were on the creeps but maybe the redhead did have something to do with it.
She certainly didn't want to get to know anyone, was she hiding out? But why? Maybe I should try and dig into these people's past. I mean after all I'm a mystery writer. I could find out who they really were.

Frank and Marjorie Bellows. I wrote their names out. Now for the redhead. I bet I could casually sift through her mail when the postman dropped it off. Of course I couldn't be seen by anyone, but funny, I don't think I'd ever seen a mailbox. Maybe she got her mail at the post office. What was I thinking? I couldn't go through her mail! I could check out the front of her house again.

As for the Bellows, just the thought of them gave me a bad taste in my mouth. I truly did not like them.
They were so pushy. I'm sure Mrs. Lane would invite them. Maybe I could try and find something out when they were here for the BBQ. But the thought of those two in my house, yuk.

I got my laptop and started searching for their names. Nothing except for an obituary in Pittsburgh for a Frank and Mary Bellows.

But they died in a car accident in 1987 and left behind two small children. They must have been young. The thought of it was saddening. Who were these two?

Same names, funny. I could pay to do an online search but I didn't even want to spend the money on them. Nope I had to talk to them and see what I could find out.

As for the mystery redhead, not sure if she would even come answer the door to Mrs. Lane if she tried to invite her. No the best approach with her would be direct, face-to-face. First I would take a walk, casually check out the redhead's house. Maybe get Mags to hear the call of nature in the front of the house. Like that would happen. Get a dog to tinkle on command. Well no time like the present to try. "Come on Mags."

I called and she came running. After hitting the buttons on the security pad, we went out the front door and down the walk. Good. Mrs. and Mrs. Creepy were nowhere to be seen.

I walked a little bit to the edge of the gated yard next door. It was a large yard I surveyed, overgrown in badly need of a cut. It was probably a grand place in its day. The big, black rod iron fence surrounded the entire house and matching stone shed. The house had ornate carvings in the stone above each window. The front door had a black rod iron looking screen door with glass instead of screen. Behind it stood a deep red front door. I guess I never stopped to see how really pretty the house was. It was surely built here before most of the houses on this road.

I was standing there staring when I looked up and there she was. Startled I just sort of jumped back a little. The red hair couldn't be missed in that upstairs window. She just stared at me. A little shaken, I tried to smile and give a little wave. Nothing. She just stared at me. Now truly, I've written about a lot of stuff in my books, creeps, killers, mystery, danger…. but this look really sort of shook me up. No return smile, no return wave, just that look. No feeling or emotion…just a cold stare. Now what to do??? Stand there and gawk? Run away?

Turning my back at this moment didn't seem like the best idea...so I just tilted my head with a look of question and stared back. She shook her head in disgust I think, and backed away from the window.

Now really, I'm trying to be nice I thought. No, I wasn't. I needed to get real, I was nosy, just plain nosy. But now there was a mystery to this woman and I intended to find out what it was. She was plain unfriendly, or hiding something. I think the latter. Off we went down the road. I would stop at Mrs. Lane's and see what she knew.

A few minutes later found me sitting in the Lane's flower garden watching the pugs chase Maggie to her delight. Mrs. Lane was pouring Lemonade again chatting about the stereo snoring she endured every night. I laughed at the thought of those two pugs like guardrails in her bed.

"Mrs. Lane, what do you know about our mystery woman next to me? She doesn't seem friendly at all, even when I wave at her." "Well dear, I don't really know anything at all except she keeps to herself. I've never seen her get mail; she has a delivery service for all her food supplies. I've seen the truck. I really don't think I've ever seen her go out. Have you?"

"Well I did bump into her as she was coming down her back stairs to the beach but she seemed annoyed and went right back up into the house when I tried to introduce myself. I'm curious. You know it must be the mystery writer in me." "Well dear, that will not deter us. I will most certainly be persistent and invite her to the neighborhood BBQ. Or at least try to." she smiled.

After a few more minutes of visiting and going over the BBQ plans and a promise to let her know if Connor and I needed anything more, Mags and I left. We walked back to our house just as Mr. and Mrs. Creepy were pulling out of their driveway.

"Come on girl let's get in the house!" I said as I ran up the steps and hurriedly keyed my code in. Inside I felt a little relief not to have had to run into them and make small talk.

After a glass of ice water and a salad, I sat down again knowing that Raeghen would want the first draft of the chapters I was working on in a few weeks. I had better get the book going again. I love writing. Loosing myself completely in my stories and characters. I was typing away when I looked up and realized Mags had to go out.

Opening the screen door out she ran. I looked up and over to the yard next door. The back patio of the big house was a little higher than my yard and there sitting outside was the redhead looking back at me again!!

Wow was this creepy or what? I stared and wait, no way, she lifted her hand just a little than put it back down. Was that a wave? She stared at me, waiting for my response? I gave a quick nod and half a smile than closed the screen door. OK, at least the ice was broken.

I could not figure out why so mysterious, reclusive. Well maybe this could be part of my book. Real life was sometimes way more interesting than fiction. We would see. For now, I had to get back to the fiction.

Chapter 9

Writing the next three chapters came easily. At this rate I would get the first draft to her next week. An early supper of salmon and salad hit the spot. Cleaning up the dishes and to the couch with hot buttered popcorn and a movie. Nestling down in the cushions I couldn't feel any more comfortable.

There was a small bit of daylight left and a warm breeze was blowing through the back screen. I was just getting into the movie when there was a loud knock on the back screen. Maggie started growling.

Uh, oh, it dawned on me I hadn't locked the back door. Maggie got up and started walking to the kitchen. I looked around for some kind of weapon. Girl! Get hold of yourself! It was just a knock. Yea a knock with my dog growling. I walked out behind her. Then I stopped surprised. There was the redhead standing at my door looking a little frantic.

"I'm sorry to bother you, but can I possibly use your phone? My cell phone is dead and all my electric just went off!" she said visibly upset. "Sure come on in." I said opening the screen door. I looked down at Mags who just sniffed her and walked back into the living room. So much for protection from her. Well she must not be a threat.

All I have is a cell phone myself but you're welcome to use it, come in the living room." I said motioning her to follow. It seemed she reluctantly followed me looking around checking out the place if I didn't know better. "It's OK, just me and Mags are here." I said hoping to calm any fears she might have about who I didn't know.

"Sorry, just a little jumpy I guess." She said as she took the cell out of my hand. "Do you mind?" she asked as she pointed back to the kitchen. "No, no, of course have some privacy." I said.

She walked back into my kitchen and all I heard was her talking low, to someone. She seemed upset by the way her voice would rise, almost pleading but I couldn't make out what she was saying and I didn't want to be obvious.

So much for the movie and popcorn bowl. She came back in and handed me the phone. "Thanks, the power company will be out in a while. I'll just go back and wait for them." she said. "Nonsense, just stay here till they come or you'll be waiting in the dark." I said nodding towards the window where the sun was setting. "It's just me and Mags here."

She looked around; again with the checking out I was sure. Maggie was totally disinterested in her so she must not be a threat. "Well, OK if you're sure."

"Of course and by the way I'm Sarah." I said. "Oh, I'm…." she was hesitating I was sure of it. I just continued to look and raised my eyebrows a little. "I'm Samantha. My friends call me Sam."

"Well, Sam, have a seat and some popcorn. I was just watching a movie. Can I get you a pop or some coffee or iced tea?" "No, no thanks anyway" she still seemed edgy. Just then Maggie started to growl again. Her eyes got big and frantic looking.

"Stay calm" I said as Mags and I walked out into the kitchen. I turned the lock on the inside door and keyed in my alarm. Why had I forgot about the alarm? I looked out the window. It had suddenly gotten dark. "What is it?" she whispered behind me.
"Not sure, but we're OK. I have an alarm system. If anyone tries to come in it will set if off and the police will be here…" I tried to assure her and myself as I said it. Maggie was still growling that low growl.

"I'm gona turn these lights off so we can see." I said as I hit the switch. I didn't know whether to let Mags out and be by ourselves or keep her in. Wait! There WAS someone outside, back by my tree. "There's someone out by the tree!" I whispered. Maggie started barking loudly now for which I was thankful.

I flipped on my backyard floodlights and the guy ran back down the beach. "What? Where?" she asked frantically.
I picked up my phone and hit the speed dial to Connor. "Who are you calling?" she asked. "Just a friend down the beach." I turned around to look at her and there with the moonlight shining in there was sheer panic on her face. "Sam, it's OK, its Connor. He's a friend it's OK."

"Sarah?" he answered, "you OK?" "Connor you'd better come up, there was someone in my backyard." I said breathlessly. "On my way." was all the reply I got. Sam was still panicking by the dining room table. I could see her pacing like a trapped animal. Then I saw Connor coming up the back taking the steps two at a time. I hit the code and unlocked the back door and he came in. Mags was jumping around glad to see him. "You OK?" he looked past me to see Sam standing there. "Anyone get hurt?"

"No we're OK Connor, just a little weirded out. This is Sam. She lives next door" I said nodding to Samantha who still had the deer in the headlights look on her. "What happened? Did you see the guy? Which way did he go?" he asked.

"I'm surprised you didn't run into him coming up the stairs. As soon as I hit those back floodlights he took off." "He probably jumped the fence and ran back down towards the A-Frames." Connor replied.

You think he was a tourist staying in the A-Frames and just nosing around?" I asked knowing better. Sure a tourist skulking around as my dad would say. He was probably one in the same who slit my screen. Like what would he want with me?

"Nah, Sarah, I'm pretty sure he's not your run of the mill tourists. But I'd sure be interested in knowing what he was doing here, and wondering if he is the same one who slit your screen" Ditto, read my mind.

"Slit your screen???" Sam asked with that same frantic voice again. "Someone tried my screen door and decided to make a big slit in it. Wouldn't have got far though with Mags here." Maggie was thoroughly enjoying the big ear rub again from Connor. Hmm, so much for protection. That didn't seem to convince Sam by the looks of her expression. Sheer terror.

"Well I think all is OK but I will look around just to be sure. Sarah make SURE you key your code in when you lock up OK? Keep your phone by you tonight. I can stay and sleep on the couch if you want if you guys are nervous." he offered. So he figured Sam was staying here. Good idea but I had already thought to offer. "Well I should be going. My lights are back on." she said staring out the kitchen window from where she stood not making a move.

"No way. I mean you don't have to go. Why don't you stay here, on the couch or the other bedroom tonight and maybe Connor can take a look around your house tomorrow to make sure no one attempted to break in there too." I said looking at Connor.
"Sure Sam, I'd be glad to. Probably good idea if your electric has been off. I can stay too Sarah, if you'd feel better."

"No its OK, we have Mags." who at the moment was on her back getting a belly rub from him. Real mean dog here. "OK "he said standing up. "I'll go back down and look around. Leave those lights on in the back for the rest of the night. Should keep anyone from nosing around." he walked to the back door and turned around.

"Nice to meet you Sam, I'll stop up in the morning and we can walk over to your house and I can check it out before you go in." He turned to me. "Don't take any chances Sarah. Lock up and key in your code OK?" He stared into my face for an extra moment. I must admit I liked that extra moment.

A lot of daydreaming went into that extra moment. A lot of what ifs. Now that surprised me. "Ok, thanks so much for coming." He gave me a smile and a squeeze on my arm and out he went.

I turned around to a dead stare from Sam. "You OK?" I asked. "You're welcome to stay. I'd probably feel a little better if you did. Besides, like Connor said, I don't think I'd want to go back over by myself."

"I don't know "she said looking around. "I should be getting back" she said staring out the window at her house. "Why did your electric go off?" I asked. "Seems funny only your house."
Again the stare. It was actually a little uncomfortable but gave me a minute to survey her. She was tall like me; a slight bit heavier and had that beautiful wild curly red hair that hung down to her shoulders. She was fair, and had dark green eyes, a great contrast to the red hair. She was actually quite striking.

"Well…." she didn't finish the sentence. "OK, then it's settled. I'll get you an extra pair of sweats. My room is right there and the spare bedroom is right across from it, unless you'd feel more comfortable on the couch."

I pointed to it. "No, no…I WILL stay if it's OK, just tonight. I guess I am a little jittery. I can stay on the couch no need to fuss with the bedroom." "Good then let me grab the sweats and you grab a couple of pops out of the fridge or lemonade or coffee, whatever you want."

I walked into the bedroom and got an extra pair out of the bottom drawer. I sensed she didn't want to be buddy buddy but she didn't want to go home alone either. Something or someone scared her into running over here when the lights went out. My bet is it was someone. I walked back into the living room as she was coming from the kitchen, Maggie following close behind her.

"Bathroom's right there." I pointed. She took the sweats and went in and changed. Sitting down on the couch she grabbed a pop and opened it still looking around the room. "I like your house. It's very comfortable, and this couch is something else" she said with half a smile.

"Yea, I like it too. Great to nestle down into and watch a movie. You interested in a movie or just talk?" I said pointing at the TV. "I'm still a little nervous…guess I won't be much of a talker or watcher." she said. I got a feeling she didn't want to talk but I'd never let that stop me. I would plow ahead ever so slowly.

"Seems like ever since I moved here there's been some excitement going on." I said. "Where are you from?" she asked. Suddenly all the memories came up, almost choking up I got out "Montana" "Wow, always wanted to go there. Lots of mountains, huh?" she said. "Yea, there are those." Suddenly I wanted to change the subject.

"Sam, some of the neighbors are going to get together here on Saturday and have a little cookout. Nothing fancy just sit around and gab. I'd love you to come." Her expression suddenly turned cold. "Well I probably won't come. I don't do well in crowds and truthfully I'm more comfortable being by myself." Well, no excuses, just a blunt reply. Actually I rather liked that about her. "Well OK, but if you change your mind just come over. Connor who you met will be here grilling and Mrs. Lane, the older woman across the street with the pugs will be here as well as some other neighbors that I don't know. Sort of a get to know you kind of thing." She turned her head and stared at the TV. "You know, if you don't mind, I'm sort of tired." she said.

"OK, I'll grab you a pillow and an afghan and we'll call it a night." Walking into the spare bedroom I grabbed two pillows off the bed and the afghan across the bottom of it and walked out and handed to them to her. I turned to go into the bedroom, Maggie following close behind. "Sarah" I heard. I turned around. "Thank you. I really am grateful you let me stay." "That's what neighbors are for." I replied smiling at her.

"Have a good sleep and I'll see you in the morning. I'll warn you though, I'm an early riser. Good Night."

Climbing into bed my mind raced with questions about her. I really knew nothing about her. I realized when I started to talk she turned the conversation around to me. Hmm that was clever. Was I imagining this? Not sure. I turned over listening to the soft snore of Mags at the bottom of the bed. I'd find out more in the morning. Or not....

Chapter 10

I woke up about 5:55AM. Trudging out in my slippers I headed to the back door to let Mags out and I noticed the empty couch and stopped. Looking back at the bathroom and spare bedroom both doors were open, quiet. Wow, she got up early and left. I went on to the kitchen and put the coffee on after letting Mags out. Staring over to her house I wondered if she wasn't nervous going in herself this morning, I would have been. Well, she said she wasn't much of a social person, I guess she was telling the truth. Better get dressed before Connor shows up. Calling Mags in and locking the door then setting the alarm, I jumped in the shower. I guess I was still a little jittery.

Getting dressed I was going over what I had to do today. Had to take part of my first draft into town and mail to Raeghen. Than to the store to pick up the last minute items for the cookout. Stop at Mrs. Lane's to go over the list. Tidy up the back yard and get extra chairs from Connor as well as the grill. I walked over to the couch and grabbed the pillows and afghan. She had folded the sweats and afghan and placed them on top of the pillows. Bending down to grab them I noticed something under the couch. Reaching down, I picked up a locket. Beautiful. Opening it I found a picture of a small girl around two or three. She was a duplicate of Sam. Was this Sam or her daughter or another relative? The resemblance was extraordinary. The knock brought me back to reality. Connor. Sticking the locket in my pocket I answered the door.

So nice to see a smiling face. I knew it was Connor as Mags never barked, just went to the door with tail wagging. "Come on in" I said as I unlocked the door. "I just stopped to walk Sam over and look around" he said looking around the room.

"You're too late. She was gone when I got up a little before six. Coffee is on. Want some?" "Sure, but what was her rush? Did she say anything last night?" he asked.

"Not a thing and it wasn't for my lack of trying" I said smiling as I handed him a hot cup of coffee. He reached for the sugar. "She changed into some sweats and that was about it. She was tired and wanted to go to bed." "Well, at least you tried. How about the BBQ? Will she come?"

He stirred his coffee. I was lost for a minute watching the coffee swirl around. "Sarah? Earth to Sarah?" "Oh," I laughed. "No interest in the BBQ either, but I left the invitation open. Maybe she'll show up."

I looked him over; dark hair, nice tan, and a brown T-shirt over some cut offs. Do they still call them cut offs? Not sure with all the new styles these days. Nice leather flip-flops. Hmm. "So I'll stop by tomorrow and bring over the grill and extra chairs for Saturday?" he asked. Nodding I came back to reality. "Sure. It's supposed to be beautiful the next several days so it will be nice. I'm not sure how many people are coming but it will be fun. I'll run into town today and pick up the odds and ends after I check with Mrs. Lane."

Now this was odd, I was actually looking forward to it. Usually I'm a bit of a recluse. But Connor was so comfortable to be around. "OK. Wonder if she asked your Mr. and Mrs. Creepy next door?"
"Oh Connor, have you seen them? She's an advertisement for way too much make up and a bad dye job …and him…have you seen that toupee??? You cannot take your eyes off it" I started laughing. He smiled.
"Can't say I've gotten that close up and personal, but yeah Mrs. Lane gave me a few small details about them. Don't know if they're coming, you have to find out."

"Well I've got to run" he said swallowing the last small amount of coffee in his cup. He set it in the sink and turned around. "Got a few things to take care of at work. I'll check with you later." He walked to the door.

"You know you can always walk down the beach tonight...maybe throw some steaks on the grill before I move it this way."

"Hmm, I'll have to think about that one. I've got to get going and mail this draft out or Raeghen will be flying out here to see what's what." "OK, see you later" he smiled as he went out the door. Mags followed him down to the beach and watched him go. She was back lying under her tree a few minutes later.

Well back to the computer. I'll finish up the draft and then walk over to Mrs. Lane's after lunch to see what was still needed for the big event. Maybe a drive into town later and maybe, just maybe, a walk down the beach.

Sitting in Mrs. Lane's backyard I was amazed all over again. Beautiful flowers everywhere. She must have two green thumbs. They were brilliant. Beautiful reds, purples, bright yellows. I could sit and stare at this forever. I guessed this must be what heaven is like. Beautiful gardens and walkways. Snort, cough, bark, and snort. Well maybe not that in heaven. I turned to see the two pugs following Maggie around bushes and flowers on the brick paths. They loved her and evidently were content to follow her as she explored.

Mrs. Lane smiled as she poured the lemonade. "I think we are ready dear. If you just pick up the buns and condiments we are good to go."

"I'll run into town after we visit for a while and get everything. You sure you don't need anything else? Connor is bringing the grill down tomorrow along with the chairs. How many people are actually coming do you know?"

I was curious if the number included Mr. and Mrs. Creepy. "Well I asked all the neighbors, well except for the house with the red haired lady. We also have an extremely discontented lady down by Connor. Betty is her name. She fights with all the neighbors, always calling the police. I didn't invite her dear. Maybe I should of" she said seeming to rethink her decision.

"Frank and Marjorie were extremely excited to come. I still say they are skulking around Sarah but we should give them the benefit of the doubt I suppose. Mark and his family, you met him when he put in the security system. I know you will like his wife. Gabby and Tony and their grand kids. A few people from church I'd like you to meet. With all the dogs and kids and adults I'd say we'll have around thirty if they all show up." "Wow and I did run into the red haired neighbor. Samantha or Sam is her name. I don't think she was too interested." I replied thinking that thirty was a lot.

"Is it OK dear? Do you think it's too many?" she seemed a little anxious. "No, no Mrs. Lane, that's fine. I've just never been too outgoing. But this will be good for me. I think it will be fine. I can just stay busy helping Connor cook." "Well there is that." she smiled and poured some more lemonade in our glasses. "Now Mrs. Lane, don't get any ideas. We're just friends." "Of course dear."

Chapter 11

The grocery store was crowded that afternoon. Finding the bread aisle, I threw in loads of buns and then pushed onto the mustard and ketchup and relish. After several bags of chips and more pop, I checked out. I think I was actually excited. I hadn't entertained in a very long time. After stopping at Tony's to grab a malt and confirm the time for Saturday, we stopped at the post office to mail my draft and then we went home.

Mags jumped out of the jeep and headed towards the gate. To my surprise it opened with a smiling Connor. "Need some help?" "Wow that was great timing. Sure!" We unloaded everything into the screened porch and sat down with a cold pop. "Well I guess we're pretty much ready except for chairs and the grill. I could probably use some help loading it into the truck." he said looking at me smiling.

"Yea sure. O K, let's go." I replied. "Oh, I just happen to have some steaks that have to be used tonight." "Sure you do." Locking up and setting the alarm, Maggie and Connor and I strolled down the beach to his house. It was actually my first time going there. I was curious to see what kind of house he had, how he decorated it.

Walking up his back steps I was pleasantly surprised. Unlike my house it looked directly at the lake without a screened porch. He had some outdoor candles lit and the steaks were marinating by the grill. Evidently he was pretty sure I'd come. "Come on in. I'll get the salad and potatoes." he said opening the sliding door. His living room was very nice. He had two leather couches that faced each other and a huge wooden coffee table in the middle. A large leather chair was at one end, and a fireplace was at the opposite end with a flat screen TV hung over it. It was very neat, clean and comfortable looking.

I followed him into the kitchen. He was taking the salad out of the fridge along with some pop. Handing me the bowl he grabbed two potatoes wrapped in foil from the oven.

"Let me grab some salad dressing and I'll be right out" he said as turned back to the fridge. I walked out to the patio to find Mags sprawled out on the stones snoring softly. Hmm make yourself at home.

He came out behind me with the dressing and potatoes. Putting them on the table he opened up the grill and turned it on. I sat down in one of the comfy chairs. The table had a large umbrella attached to it and three other chairs. The plates and silverware were already on it. He grabbed a pop and opened it. "Hope you're hungry." "Actually I am. Your view is gorgeous. I know we look at the same lake but I have the porch. I mean I like the porch but I like your patio too." I said looking around.

"Yeah, I'm pretty happy with it. I was glad when I finally moved out here from town. There some issues here too, though. I'm not sure any place is perfect. One of my neighbors is not a happy camper, but other than that it's really nice." "Yeah I think Mrs. Lane told me about her." I replied opening the other pop.
"I never figured it out," he said putting the steaks on the grill. "Some people are never happy; she's always calling the police about this neighbor or that. It gets old. So changing the subject, do you think you're ready for Saturday and the big BBQ?"

"I think so. The whole thing surprises me. Lately I've not been really into gatherings. A lot of people." "Why Sarah?" he asked. His question surprised me. I did not want to go into any explanation about Montana. "Oh I don't know. I'm just more comfortable keeping to myself "I said with him staring intently at me. "The steaks need turning."
 I replied changing the subject from myself." "Hmm, you sure that's the only reason?" he asked. He continued to look at me for a few more seconds before tending to the steaks. I nodded.

They were delicious. I love steak. He had sautéed some mushrooms in butter and piled them on top. It was a glorious meal and I told him so. We sat back and watched the sun set while Maggie happily chewed on the steak bones.

We made plans to bring the grill down to my house and start setting up around noon so we wouldn't have a lot to do Saturday. He had something to take care of Friday morning so the later time would work better for him.

We strolled back to my house with Maggie leading the way. He walked me up to the screened porch and waited while I keyed in the alarm buttons. Thanking him I squeezed his hand and smiled and walked in. He turned around and went back down the stairs. Mags went directly in front of the couch and lay down. Contented she was snoring within minutes.

Changing into sweats I nestled down in the couch and thought about the coming event. I had met most everyone except a few friends of Mrs. Lane's from church. Church friends. That was OK. I was raised on the pews. My mom saw to that. I was comfortable around Christians. I just wasn't comfortable talking to or about God these days. Feeling disappointed in Him I knew was dangerous for me. I need to pour out my heart to Him and get on with it, but I just wasn't ready to let go of Caleb just yet or the blame I threw God's way. Or was I?
Why the excitement of seeing Connor? These were things that needed thinking about, but I didn't want to do that now. I sort of didn't want to think at all.

Bang! A loud crash outside got Maggie storming the back door barking wildly. What was going on now??? Again?? I flipped off the lights and ran to the kitchen. Peeking out the window I couldn't see anything. But something crashed. Maggie was still barking madly…let her out? Or keep her in? I figured letting her out would run someone off so I keyed the pad and unlocked the door just as I flipped on the outside lights.

The whole backyard lit up instantly and someone went running down the back steps with a wild angry dog right on their heels. I hit speed dial. "Sara, miss me already huh?" Connor said laughing. "Connor, Mags is after someone outside!" I yelled in the phone. "On my way!" he said back.

I continued to look out and could see lights being flipped on next door in Sam's house. I couldn't hear Mags anywhere and now I was getting nervous. Then I heard a gunshot and yelping. No!!! I took off out the door in a dead run and ran straight into Connor. "Stay back!" he said. He took off back down the steps and took the fence with a leap in the air. No way was I staying back. I followed suit although I had to climb over. I went running down the beach in the direction of the A-Frames.

I could see Connor ahead in the moonlight and then he stopped and knelt down. Oh No! Not Mags! I rushed up to him out of breath. "Connor!!" I yelled. "She's OK Sarah, just nicked her. Someone sure the heck didn't want her in pursuit." He picked her up quietly sweet- talking into her ear. She licked his face.

We went back up to my house using the gate this time and took her inside. In the light I could see no damage except a scrape where the bullet must have slid right past her shoulder. I was shaking as I said a small prayer of thanks.

 "She's OK, but if it would make you feel better we could get hold of the vet" he said as he was dialing his phone. "Well, if you're sure it's OK; you don't have to call him."

 He continued to dial and walked into the kitchen. I could hear his voice rise…but to who? Out he walked. "Just got hold of the police Sarah. They are gona patrol around your house tonight. I'm not leaving so if you have an extra pillow I'd appreciate it."

"What do you mean?" "Sarah! Someone had a gun and shot at Maggie as she chased them down your yard! That's what I mean. I don't know what's going on here but you are NOT going to be alone tonight." He stared at me and I gave up knowing there was no use. To be truthful, I would feel a little safer with Connor there and Maggie out of commission. I went and got a pillow and afghan and sat down on the other end of the couch.

He grabbed us two pops out of the fridge and sat down facing me. "What's going on Sarah?" "What do you mean? I don't know who that was or why all of this stuff is happening to me. I just moved here! I don't even know anyone except a few people. And I really don't think Mrs. Lane or Tony or even Mrs. and Mrs. Creepy would want to do me in. As for Sam next door, she seems freaked out as it is, don't think she is too concerned with me. You tell me. What do you think is going on? Why the target on my back?" I asked him suddenly wondering about him. I realized I really didn't know too much about Connor.

He stared at me as I went over in my mind everything that happened. The flowerpots, the slit screen, the guy the other night, now another intruder, this time with a gun. "Well?" he asked. "Well what?" I found myself angrily replying.
 "What Connor, do you think I'm running a drug ring or some other kind of crime racket here? These things are happening to me! And I have no idea what is going on!"

"Why did you move Sarah?" he asked softly. I stared at him. What was this, the third degree? I refused to answer the question in any detail. "That's my business." I said just as quiet. I stared back. We seemed to be in a deadlock. I was indignant thinking I was getting fifty questions and I had no idea as to why all this stuff happened and by the way, who was he to ask all the questions? The truth be known; I didn't know too much about him either.

I told him I was tired and headed to the bedroom and closed the door. Mags chose to stay in the living room. I got undressed and got in bed my mind going over and over all the events. It was crazy, all the stuff going on.

I lived next to Mr. and Mrs. Creepy and didn't know anything about them. Well, maybe it was time I started to take control of the situation. I planned on getting all the info I could from them and everyone else including Connor. I knew nothing about any of them but that was gona change!

I fumed lying there in bed, mad at myself that it had gotten so out of control. I had promised myself years ago that no one would ever have control of my life but me. I wasn't even sure why I was so mad at Connor. Maybe it was me I was mad at. I had let my guard down, feeling too comfortable and getting quite social. Did I think I was a social butterfly or something?? I had been keeping to myself since Caleb died. Maybe I should just go back to that. But then I could hear my mom in my head…" Sarah, remember God has a plan, it's gona be wild, it's gona be a ride. Sit back and just wait to see what it is!"

Well mom, this didn't seem like a good plan if that's what this was, I thought. I couldn't wrap my thoughts around why I was so upset. I did not want to have feelings for Connor, was this what this was?

Divine appointments, my mom would tell me. When God puts two people together for a specific reason. Was this a divine appointment? With Connor? But a gun; someone had fired a gun at my dog. Were they gona use it on me??? That made me mad and I knew I should have been scared if I had any sense.

I got up and quietly opened the door. Heading towards the kitchen for a glass of water I glanced at the couch. The moonlight shone in through the windows and Connor was softly snoring. No shirt, just a pair of jeans and shoeless.
I stopped and watched for a few seconds then headed on to the kitchen. I was as quiet as could be as I poured the water. Turning around I dropped the glass startled.

"What???" He stood in the doorway with that amused smile again saying nothing. I hadn't even heard him get up. "What ya doing Sarah?" "Connor! You scared me! I thought you were asleep. I was getting a glass of water and now see what you made me do!" as I bent down and started to pick up the glass. Thank goodness it was hard plastic. I grabbed a towel and wiped up the floor. He still stood smiling at me. "Well what?" I demanded.

"It's getting late, try to get some rest. I'm not going anywhere." he said as he turned back to the living room and promptly made himself comfy on my couch. Still Mags didn't move. Poor thing. The grazing of the bullet…uh oh…the bullet. I forgot for a second, the whole incident. I stood still and looked blankly at him. "You just remembered what happened tonight didn't you?" he asked.

"Yea" I said quietly. "What is going on Connor? Why would someone be after me? For what reason? I left Montana to leave behind bad memories. That's all." He looked at me for a few seconds, seeming to contemplate what to say. "OK" was all I got.

I shrugged my shoulders and went towards the bedroom. "We'll work it out Sarah. Don't worry. Maybe it's not you they're after anyway, if they're after anyone. We don't know. We've notified the police and you're pretty secure here, well your guard dog is a little down and out right now, but it's just a graze and she should be up and at it in no time." he seemed to try and assure me. "Thanks" I said as I went in and shut the door.

Chapter 12

I woke up to the sound of Connor talking on the phone and the smell of breakfast. I got up and listened at the door. It was a little muffled so I tried to crack the door without him hearing me.

"Check it out! I mean it! I don't want her getting hurt! Run down a list of who in the family could be out here and get back to me." What? Who was he? Who was he talking to? I watched him go back to the frying pan on the stove.

That's what I smelled. Bacon. I walked out as if I didn't hear anything, but what was that all about? Was he a good guy or band guy? Now I was suspicious of Connor. Mags was sitting up next to him and he was talking to her. "You're a good girl Mags, protecting her. I've got a few slices of bacon here with your name on them."

"You spoil her." I said walking over to the coffee pot after petting her. "She deserves it! She took a bullet for you, so to speak" he leaned down rubbing her behind the ears again.
 Always the ears. "So I'm gona finish breakfast and then I have to run into town. When I get back I'll bring over the chairs and grill and the stuff for the kids. That sound good?" he asked as he slid the bacon pieces on my plate.

"Great" was all I could say while chewing some bacon and grabbing the plate of eggs. We talked while we ate and then he helped me wash the dishes up and off he went. Taking a long hot shower sounded good and that's just what I did. I felt so much better.

Raeghen called, wanting an update on the book and I spent an hour on the phone with her. After assuring her all was right with the world, and I did send the draft, I hung up and went outside.

Mags walked out slowly and went and lay in her usual spot under the tree. Fresh air and sun would help. I straightened up the patio and surveyed the yard. One of the selling points besides the porch was the yard. It was huge and sloped down to the beach. I did love this place. It was comfortable and inviting.

I took out the little lawn mower and mowed the grass the best I could. It took a while as my yard was huge. I had planted flowers in the pots that stood around the patio when I first came, and now they were in full bloom and beautiful. No competition for Mrs. Lane's backyard but nice as well. I was pleased at how it all looked.
I grabbed more chairs out of the storage shed and put them around the other tree. It was going to be a beautiful day and I was content as I turned towards Samantha's house. I wondered if she would come.

I started down the sloping yard to the gate on the beach. Knowing Mags was resting I closed it behind me and walked till I came to her steps. I started up slowly wondering if she would come out. I saw an upstairs drape move out of the corner of my eye and I continued on. Reaching her landing I noticed a small patio table with a couple of chairs that stood off to the side. A book was on the table. No grill, no other furniture.
I looked at the door and it opened. Sam looked out both ways as she opened it a crack. "Hi Sarah, what do you want?"

Well, that was to the point. Can't say she beats around the bush. "I just wanted to remind you of the BBQ tomorrow. Just neighbors. I'd love you to come Sam." I stared at her waiting for the reply. "Thanks Sarah for letting me stay the other night. Guess I just got a little spooked." She stared back. "Of course. That's what neighbors are for. If every you need anything…" I started. "I don't." she said flatly and closed the door. O K, well that went well. I thought I should be upset with her rudeness but I wasn't as I walked away.

I rather liked her. A lot of mystery surrounded her but that's what I loved…. a mystery. Anyways, she was another on my list to find out about.

I went back and checked on Mags and went in the house to get a cold pop. I could get in another couple of chapters but today I didn't want to. Maybe I would be human bait. I grabbed my water can and walked out the front door. Good, Mrs. Creepy was in the front yard. I puttered around in the flowers and banged my can till I was sure she saw me.

"Hello there! "she yelled waving her hat. I mean we were right next door to each other, not like she had to yell across the block. "Oh, hi, I guess I didn't see you." I lied, hoping my mom was still praying for me. "Were you both going to be able to come to the BBQ tomorrow?" I asked, dreading that meeting but determined to find out some info.
"Oh of course! We wouldn't miss it for the world!" she said happily. I bet you wouldn't, Mrs. Snoopy. "Well that's great; say around three or four...that's what Mrs. Lane thought." "We will be there!" she replied through ruby red fat lips. She had tons of blue eye shadow on. Didn't people look in the mirrors before they went out? The bleached blonde hair was ratted high on her head with a red bow right in the center. Horrible. "Great! Will it just be the two of you?" already knowing the answer.

She looked at me rather oddly for a second and then gathered herself. "Yes, just Frank and myself."
"OK, I will see you tomorrow, got to go, lots to do." I said as I opened the front door and went in. Well nothing there. Maybe I could talk a little more tomorrow although I really couldn't stand either of them. I was walking through the kitchen when there was a knock on the back door. It was Connor. "Hey Sarah, I was gona run the truck down with the grill and chairs if now is OK?"

Opening the door, I let him and Maggie in at the same time. She promptly lay down on her bed, and he sat down at the table. "All OK here?" he asked staring at me intently. Brown eyes. "Sure daylight seems to give you courage, go figure." I replied smiling at him. "Don't get too brave Sarah. There was still a guy with a gun."

He looked serious as he stared at me. "I know Connor; I don't want to think of it too much; we have a party to plan."

"I'll go back down the beach and load up, you want to come?" We went out the backdoor and down the steps with Maggie following a little slowly. We chatted about the A-Frames and the tourists who spent summers there, Samantha, what her story might be and Maggie.

When we got to his house he backed his truck up and leaned a long, wide board against the tailgate. We pushed the huge grill up with little trouble and then the chairs. The stuff for the kids was in one big box and we slid that in at the end.
 Sliding the board in the pickup bed, we got Maggie in the truck and headed back to my place.

Unloading was easy. We helped Maggie out of the truck and she went over to her tree and lay down. She was getting back to her old self but it could take a couple of more days of rest. We set up the net and positioned the grill. He had lots of grilling utensils so he must not be new at this.

"You feel like taking a little ride? I'll show you some sights." I looked up. "Sure." We left Maggie sleeping under her tree and got in the truck and started out towards town, taking a left. "The beach down here is Grand Mere. A lot of it has washed away but still some nice little spots to fish in the little ponds around.
 There are a lot of sub divisions that have gone up in the past few years, but it's still pretty nice," he said as he drove.

 He kept looking in his mirror so much that I finally looked in my side mirror to see a black sedan following us. "Trouble?" I asked. He turned and stared at me for a few seconds, before he answered. "Not sure, but we're gona find out." He sped up and so did the sedan. I grabbed the handle rest on the door knowing this may not turn out well. We were on a paved road that soon turned into dirt the closer we got to the shore. We left a pretty big cloud of dust and dirt behind us as Connor sped faster.

I kept looking at my mirror and turning around. Sure enough, the sedan was staying right on our trail. "Hold on Sarah, this could get a little rough." With that being said, he jerked the truck left, down a little two track road and the sedan slammed on its breaks as it slid by.

Connor took the opportunity to make a quick U-turn and headed back the way we came. My breathing came faster as the truck speed rose and we drove back the way we just came. I couldn't see the sedan as we left a huge cloud of dust.
 We hit the paved road and Connor floored it. I held on tight as the wind blew my hair all over. I didn't want to let go to roll the window up and Connor was intent on driving. I felt like we were on a racetrack and then it hit me. WHO was chasing us and why? Police would have turned on lights and a siren. This couldn't be good.

"Hold on!" he yelled. I braced myself and the truck slammed to a stop. He pulled over. The sedan sped by. I could only see one man, the driver. What was going on? I wasn't as scared as I was mad. This was getting to be too much. I turned and stared at him saying nothing. "Let's go back."

"No! Connor what is going on? Who was that? Why was he following us? I'm still reeling from the gunshot that almost killed Maggie and you say let's go back like nothing's wrong."
He pulled the truck out on the road not speaking. "Let's get something to eat." He drove into St. Joe to a little drive in. I had Let's hope my appetite came back. He parked and we walked in. Walking in was like walking back into time. The Jukebox was in the corner playing Motown. I was in heaven. I sat down in a booth as he went up to order.

 This place was crazy! Old, small records were hung all over the wall. Pictures from the fifties hung everywhere. I loved it. He came back with a smile on his face. "I knew you'd like this place. It's my favorite besides Tony's

. They have the best hamburgers with a little surprise." He looked so good, dark tan, big smile, extremely white teeth. O K back to reality. "So what do you think is going on? You never answered me Connor."

"Well not really sure Sarah. Either you have someone after you or they have you wrong and think you're someone else." he said. "What? Who" I don't know anybody who people would be aft…" I stopped mid-sentence and stared. Samantha.

"You don't think it could be Samantha do you? Why she doesn't even look like me." I searched his face. No expression. "Well?" I asked again. "Connor, your order is ready hon," A heavyset lady yelled from the counter.
He got up and exchanged a few works and laughs with the woman he apparently knew if she was on a first name basis with him. Full of surprises.

"OK, take a bite and let me know," he said as he handed me a burger, fries and a large coke. I unwrapped the burger, huge as it was, and took a bite. What? What was the taste? It was delicious! Olives! I opened up the hamburger and look inside. Green olives covered the burger. "This is superb! Delicious! I love it!" Spending the next few minutes feeding my face with the burger and eating fries, I almost forgot the conversation. We talked about how he discovered the place by accident and how good the food was. Then our conversation took a serious note.

"So what do you think of this whole thing? You never told me," I asked. He chewed up the burger and grabbed a napkin. "Not sure Sarah, but something's definitely up and you seem to be right in the center of things."

He wiped his mouth and took a drink before he continued. "I really think you'd better be careful till we can figure this out." I ate another fry trying to sort everything in my head. "But what if Samantha is involved somehow?" I asked grasping at straws.

"I'm not sure how but you need to be careful. Let's get back and get the stuff ready for tomorrow." He stood up collecting the wrappers and we went out the door. We drove back slowly and he talked about his family. His parent's had both been teachers. His dad passed away two years ago and his mom lived near his sister Tia in Indiana. Not too far away. I was glad he shared it with me. We arrived at my house and Mags was still sleeping. She raised up to see us walk in and lay back down.

We set out a couple of coolers on the porch, which we'd fill with ice and pop tomorrow. We stacked the paper plates, cups and utensils on the table inside the porch. We put the buns and chips next to them. Done. "Well, we're good to go I think." he said. "I agree." I said smiling. "Want to go for a boat ride? My boat is big enough we can take Maggie and put her in the cabin downstairs." "Great! I'd love to see the sun set on Lake Michigan, especially on the water." What? I couldn't swim. Was I nuts? But it did sound like fun.

Locking up we went down the beach with Maggie following slowly. He ran up to his house and got the keys and we got on the boat. I was impressed. Nice boat, with a small cabin below. It had a mini kitchen and table and slept four.

He started the boat and we backed slowly away from the dock and went out. Connor drove slowly; maybe he could see I was definitely not a water person. I was gripping the sides of the boat so hard my knuckles were white. "Sarah, you can relax. I'm really a good boater. I won't go fast. We'll go around the pier and look at the boardwalk."

"Just remember Connor, I'm from Montana. Not a lot of big lakes there, well a few, but I haven't been on them and I can't swim." Flashback. Actually I had. I was on the Flathead Lake near Polson Montana with Caleb. We had gone on a Blues Cruise. It had been fun with the music and food.

Circling the lake, we had looked at all the beautiful homes and daydreamed. Stop it. O K back to the present.

I looked up to see him staring at me. "You OK?" he asked. "Yeah, just some memories." I smiled back. He didn't say anything but just nodded. We went around the pier. There were still a lot of people fishing. I was never a big fisherman when I grew up but maybe I should give it a try.

I went down in the cabin to check on Maggie and she had made herself comfortable on the bed. Sound asleep. "She OK?" Connor asked when I came back up. "Yeah, I know I'm overly protective but she's been with me for a while and I'm pretty attached." "I know. I lost my dog last year and couldn't bear to get another. I had a Rottweiler, Sasha. She was scared of everything, especially thunder. But I loved her and she was a great dog."

We cruised slowly past Silver Beach, which had a massive set of lights along the shore. Looking up on the bluffs we could see St. Joe. It was beautiful. Numerous people were sitting on blankets on the shore. They waved as we went by. We waved back.
 I thoroughly enjoyed myself. I soon forgot I had no idea how to swim. I could only hope there was no sudden monster wave tipping us over.

We cruised towards a bridge, which separated St. Joseph and Benton Harbor. We turned around slowly and went back the way we came. We were now in the moonlight with our boat light shining the way. It was a fantastic night. "Boy Connor, you could get lost in all those stars." I said as I pointed upwards to the sky. He nodded. "I come out here every time I'm stressed, just take a ride and it relaxes me." "I can see why."

Pulling up to his dock was a little depressing. I didn't want the night to end but we did have a big day tomorrow with the BBQ.
 He walked us back and I locked up and got ready for bed.
 I thought about all who was coming. I was extremely curious about Mr. and Mrs. Creepy next door. Especially after my Internet search. Had they taken over some identities?

They did have the same names as a dead couple. I put nothing past them. I would see what I could find out tomorrow.

As far as Samantha was concerned, I decided she probably wouldn't come. Too many people. I still had the locket. Why hadn't I given it back? There would be a time to do that. A time to find out a little more. Connor. What WAS his story? I realized I still really didn't know too much about him. He did tell me a little about his family but what about work? What exactly did a consultant for power plants do? And why no time schedule. Didn't regular working people have regular hours? I knew I was very fortunate to get to stay home and do my job. I loved that; but all of these questions need answers and tomorrow I would start.

Chapter 13

Morning came quickly. I had tossed and turned going over all that had happened. I still didn't have any answers. Well I would just be downright nosy today! After a hot shower and throwing on shorts and a tank top, I decided to walk down to Connors and see when he was gona come over. It was a beautiful morning and I was sure he must be up by now. As I got to his stairs and looked up, I stopped. A slender girl about thirty was standing on the patio.

I watched as he came out the door laughing and walked over and embraced her. I can't say I wasn't a little shocked. I turned around and started walking back to my house. I'm so stupid! Of course I should have known there would be other women. How dumb was I to fall for the guy? Was that was happened? Did I actually have feelings? I was mad at myself as my phone started ringing. I looked at it: Connor. I didn't answer.

I walked back and went upstairs. I started cleaning the house. If company was coming I wanted it spotless; besides, when you're upset cleaning is the best thing. It's amazing what you get done! I had done all the dishes and cleaned the kitchen and was just finishing the bathroom where there was a knock on the back door.
I went into the kitchen to see Connor standing there. I just looked at him. "Sarah, I thought I saw you and Maggie walk down the beach. I called but you didn't answer." he said. I just looked at him. "I left my phone at home." My response was pretty flat line. He just looked at me. "There was someone I wanted you to meet." "Connor, I'm sorry, I'm pretty busy right now. We have people coming over remember?"

I admit my reply was pretty cold. He stared at me for a few seconds. "OK, well I'll see you later" he said quietly as he walked off. Meet? Seriously? Like I want to meet someone you're dating I thought. The next few hours I was pretty busy. I filled the coolers with ice and pop and started setting all the condiments out. I got everything I could think he would use for grilling. I had chairs and tables set up all over the yard. I must say I was pretty pleased with how it all looked.

I looked at the clock. It was already two and people would be coming in a couple of hours. I took Maggie in and locked the door and took a nice long bath. Relaxing in the tub I started to feel pretty bad as to how I treated Connor. There was nothing between us romantically so why was I so upset? I really wasn't ready to get involved again so soon after Caleb. I made up my mind to be extra nice to him and his date.

I got out of the bath and put on some fresh clothes. I put together two huge fruit salads and just finished washing up when a knock on the front door interrupted my thoughts. I opened it to snorting and kisses and Mrs. Lane. I started laughing. "Come on in you guys!! So glad to see you Mrs. Lane. I think I'm already." Monty and Tilly plowed on in, in their usual way, to Maggie's delight. A few races around the couch and dining room table and they settled down. I let them out the back door to the yard and they went around exploring the tables and chairs. I tuned on the music in the living room and was glad I had speakers out in the porch. Music drifted outside as we visited and took food out to the table.

On the third trip out, I looked up to see Connor and his friend come up the steps. Be nice, I told myself. "Connor. So nice to see you!" said a beaming Mrs. Lane. "Hi Mrs. Lane, let me help you with that" he said as she took a tray of condiments from her. "I can see the pugs are ready to meet and greet," he laughed as Monty bit the top of his sandal with affection and Tilly tried to climb up his leg. The "friend" just stood there smiling looking absolutely beautiful in her little red sundress.

"I want you to meet my little sister Tia," he said as he proudly hugged her. Sister? Sister! Tia? Of course! He told me about her. Was I relieved? No way. I don't think I was...? "Tia, so nice to meet you my dear." said Mrs. Lane.

He looked at me with that smile again and I stuck out my hand. "I've heard a lot of nice things about you Tia, I'm Sarah." She smiled as she grasped my hand and gave it a quick squeeze. "As I have about you too Sarah." she said with a big smile.

We finished setting up and Connor started the grill as our guests started to come. Tony and Gabby and Mark and his wife were the first guests. It was nice to meet Mark's wife and kids and everybody seemed to know everybody else. Church maybe? Tia made herself right a home. I was glad. She was always smiling and so pretty. I could see the resemblance when Connor stood by her side at the grill. I smiled.

"Happy Dear?" I heard Mrs. Lane bend down and speak quietly in my ear as I sat in a chair by the grill. I turned around and smiled. "Yea, I guess so." "Ever hear of divine appointments dear?" she smiled as she walked away. No way! This was starting to get strange. That was exactly what my mom would say. I smiled and shook my head.

Monty started barking as the next set of guests to arrive. The Bellows, Frank and Marjorie. I think Monty might have been overcome by the sight of those two, I know I was! Marjorie came first. Her bleached blonde hair was ratted high on her head with a bright purple bow right in the middle of it.
There are truly no words to describe this sight. She had some deep purple eye shadow on and heavy eyeliner around her eyes. The mascara was so thick it had smudged under her eyes. Not at all becoming, but that wasn't the best. She had a frilly white blouse on with some bright yellow pants. A pair of jewel-studded slippers were on her feet. Her toes were painted fire engine red. She had tons of costume jewelry on and long balls on chains hung from her ears. She was quite a site.

Frank followed right behind. He had some checked pants on with a tight shirt on. Too tight. He should have chosen the next two sizes bigger. I wonder if he could breathe in that shirt. Topping it all off was the "rug" on his head. Oh my gosh, you could not take your eyes off of it. It was blonde to match his wife's hair!

He must have a variety of colors; it was so bad all I could do was stare with my mouth open.

"Close your mouth, you're gawking." I heard Connor say behind me. I turned around just horrified. "Do you see?" I asked trying not to burst out laughing. He was trying to avert his eyes and I don't know how long we could hold it in. The sight of the two of the, well you can't imagine it in your wildest dreams!

I heard Mrs. Lane greeting them and introducing them around. When she got to us she nodded our way. "You know Sarah and Connor don't you? This is Connor's sister Tia." she said. "Hello there." Frank said as Marjorie stood behind him like one of those bobble dolls. He had a huge unlit cigar in his hand. "Please don't smoke that here Frank; there are a lot of kids and dogs around." "Okay Missy, whatever you say" he said and put it in his pocket. They just stood there and stared. Uncomfortable!

"So tell me Frank, are you and your wife retired?" Connor asked. As always, he seemed calm, cool, collected, not at all embarrassed to ask questions. "Ah yes, why yes we are." said Frank clearly uncomfortable. "Where did you live before here?" asked Connor. I couldn't believe he was so direct. "Well, many places young man, many places. Just liked the beach is all. Come on Marj, let's get something to drink." and off he walked.

I started smiling and nudged Connor. "I can't believe you." "What? You wanted to know didn't you? But we still didn't find out anything." He put some hamburgers on the grill. More and more people came and it seemed most everyone knew everyone else. Everyone was so nice. I was really having a good time. The kids were playing and some of the adults took them down to the beach. Tia, Mrs. Lane and I saw to the refreshments and made sure everyone was eating. It was a great time.

I looked over to Samantha's house several times to see if she changed her mind, but she didn't.

I went into the house to get some more napkins and heard someone whispering. I walked down the hall and found Frank and Marjorie in my bedroom! "Can I help you?" I asked coldly. They turned around quickly and looked like a mouse caught in a trap.
"Ah we just got the wrong door, we were looking for the bathroom." he said with sweat forming on his forehead. Again Marjorie just bobbed her head up and down in agreement.

I stared at them and got that uncomfortable feeling again. "It's not in here." I said. "Yea, yea we can see that. Let's go Marj." They walked out quickly through the living room and out the porch door. "Bathroom huh?" I said out loud to no one in particular and shut both bedroom doors.

Connor walked in right then and stopped and looked at me. "What's up?" he asked. "I just found Mr. and Mrs. Creepy going through my bedroom, that's what's up." I said. "Are you kidding me? Do you want me to go have a talk with those two?" he asked visibly angry. "No, Connor. Just let it go. I'm not through trying to get info from them yet. They still have some information in them I'll bet you that." "OK but we'll keep a close eye on them. If either comes in here one of us will be right behind."

We walked back out and went back to the grill and our party. I suddenly heard a laugh I knew and turned around to see blonde hair blowing in the breeze. Hannah!!! She was talking to Mrs. Lane and smiling. I ran over and hugged my friend.

"When did you get in? How is Heda? Could you leave her? How long can you stay?" I asked so surprised and glad to see my old friend. A familiar face. "Oh Sarah, you're the same as ever." she laughed and hugged me back.

"Heda's daughter came to stay a few days and I thought why not a long weekend to see you. So here I am!" Hannah was always smiling. That is what I liked best about her.

I always felt good around her. After introductions to everyone and Maggie jumping wildly at our old friend, we sat down at a table with a couple of plates.

" I just wanted to see your place and make sure you were OK. You know me. I can't be comfortable unless I know you're OK." She reached over and squeezed my hand. She was my person. That friend who knows everything about you and still loves you in spite of it. You don't find many friends like her. I told her everything that had happened and I could see her eying Connor.

"What about him?" she asked raising her eyebrows. "We are just friends Hannah. He lives a couple houses down the beach and is always there if I need him." "Hmm" was all she said. She smiled at me and told me how things were going back home.
Events at churches and the boutique.

"How long can you stay?" "Well, Heda's daughter is leaving on the morning flight Monday, so I thought I'd fly back Monday night in case Heda needs anything. Just a few days' friend." "I'll take it." I said happy to see her again. The party lasted till about ten that night with everyone just sitting around and talking.
I couldn't believe how well I enjoyed myself. Hannah and Tia got along great and talked and laughed on the porch swing.

 Connor and I watched them from the grill. "I like your friend. She seems really nice." he said. "She is and I'm so glad she came even if it's only a few days."

"Well, after you get caught up, maybe tomorrow the four of us can go for a boat ride. Maybe show her some sights, unless you want to spend time alone with her." he said very thoughtful. "That sounds like a great idea! I'll tell her."

We made plans to get together at his house the next day, later in the afternoon. That gave us the morning to get the yard back to normal, but after looking around, there wasn't much to do.

Everyone had helped clean up. I was so surprised. Connor said he'd get the grill and the rest of the items on Monday. We could use the grill if we wanted to over the weekend. I never saw when Frank and Marjorie left but I was glad they had.

Hannah and I said good-bye to Tia and Connor and walked Mrs. Lane to her house along with the pugs. She flipped on her back lights and showed Hannah the garden. Needless to say, she was very impressed. She invited us to church the next day and Hannah looked like she wanted to accept, but I made excuses that we only had a day and a half together so we would pass.

All and all it was such a great ending to a great day. We walked back and talked and talked till at least two that night. I locked the doors and set the alarm and we hit it. Morning would come too quickly. I said a small prayer of thanks that my friend had come. After everything that had happened the last few days it was nice to have a familiar face.

Chapter 14

Morning came all too sudden. We had stayed up talking and catching up. On what I'm not sure, because we talk regularly on the phone and Skype but I was so glad to have her with me. We had a late breakfast of French toast on the porch with our coffee. I saw Sam come out on her back porch and waved, but she just went back in her house. "Not too friendly is she?" Hannah asked. "No not really. I'm trying to get to know her but she's not trying back. I think there's a story to her."

"Well, it won't be long before you figure it out Sarah and have her in your next book." she laughed. We cleaned up and took showers and then went down to the beach with Mags.
 We sat on a blanket for another couple of hours and talked and talked. Finally, around four Connor called and invited us for the boat ride he had mentioned the night before. We grabbed some jackets and filled a small cooler with goodies for the ride. We got Maggie and started to walk down the beach to Connors. She was getting back to her old self, running in the waves and barking at them. Tia and Connor were just coming down his steps
as we approached.

"You sure there's nothing between you two Sarah? He is so nice and so is his sister." Hannah said as she looked at them and waved. "Hannah, stop." I said but I wondered if I didn't agree. The four of us got on board along with Maggie and started out. Tia and Hannah were sitting in the front chatting up a storm while Maggie found her way below and got on the bed. We cruised the opposite way from the pier for quite a while before I unpacked the cooler and set out some pops, cheese, crackers and fresh veggies and dip.

The weather was just right. He turned the motor off and we just drifted. We all ate and talked like old friends. Hannah told them how I didn't know how to swim and coaxed Connor to teach me. "She is deathly scared of water I tell you. I'm surprised you got her in the boat." she told him laughing.

We were having such a good time when I looked up to see Connor staring intently behind us. I turned around to see a speedboat approaching quite fast with two guys in it. It was coming straight at us. "Get down!" Connor shouted. The three of us were a little surprised at him and just sat and looked at him until he yelled again. "Get down NOW!"

We all hit the deck like you'd see in a movie. It sped by so fast and so close the spray covered us all. He got up and was clearly angry. "What's going on?" Tia asked. "Not sure but we're not taking any chances. Sarah's had too many close calls lately."
He said as he steered the boat ahead. He picked up his cell and called the coast guard to report the boat. We just looked at each other. "Connor do you think you're overreacting?" Tia asked.

"NO" he stated flatly. She looked at us and shrugged her shoulders. "Connor, let's take Hannah and Tia back over by Silver Beach to see the carousel from the water." I said trying to lighten the mood. He nodded, still serious, and turned back toward the beach. Ever so slowly we went staying closer to the shore than we had been.

It was just starting to get dusk out. It was relaxing in the boat. We cruised down the shore of St. Joseph and looked at all the houses on the bluff. We approached the pier and watched all the fishermen still out there.

Hannah gasped when she saw the lit carousel. It was quite a sight, people walking up and down the boardwalk and the merry-go-round all lit up. We couldn't hear its music from the boat but it was pretty neat anyway.

Connor suggested docking and walking up the stairs to the town of St. Joe to get a late bite to eat. We all agreed and set out. We took Maggie with us, as there were numerous outside tables at the restaurants. We found one and all sat down. We decided to split a pizza and sat and talked and talked. It was really a lot of fun. The ice cream place was calling our names so off we went.

Connor and Hannah went in and Tia and I stayed with Mags. "So Sarah, what do you think of Connor?" asked Tia point blank. "Well talk about being blunt Tia." I laughed and she did too. "That was sort of blunt wasn't it? But …what do you think? I think you guys make a great couple!" she said. "Oh Tia, I'm not sure about that. We're just friends. He is a great guy and all but I don't know…" I left it hanging. "So what happened Sarah?" she asked quietly. Suddenly my eyes filled with tears at the thought of Caleb. I was surprised, as so much time had passed.

"I lost someone suddenly. He was shot." I was surprised again that I said that. "It will get better Sarah in time." she said as she squeezed my arm. I looked up to see Connor and Hannah standing there. Connor was staring intently at me like he missed something, which in fact he did, but I had no intention of explaining. They handed us our cones and we strolled down the street.
It was such a beautiful night. Hannah and Tia walked with Maggie chatting like old friends as Connor and I strolled behind.

It was a comfortable silence between us. I liked that. Not having to keep a conversation going about needless things. You talked when you felt like it and the other person understood. No pressure.

We got to the end of the street and sat on benches listening to music coming from one of the bars. It was a unique town.
On each corner there was a large carving. Pirates, Clowns, boats etc. The kids loved it and I think the adults did too as there were pictures being taken on each corner. We watched as the tourists strolled by. Several stopped to pet Maggie and she loved it. Such a ham. We started back to the boat after a while and walked down the stairs to the boardwalk. The carousel was still going and the four of us decided to ride!

Maggie was content to sit and be tied to a bench with a little girl around four and her grandma. Both loved on her while we rode. She ate it up. She was always so friendly to everyone.

I grabbed a giraffe and Hannah a bear. Tia chooses a horse and Connor a whale. We laughed and laughed and took pictures of each other with our phones. We strolled on back to the boat and started back. It was a great time.

We docked at his house and decided to walk back to ours for coffee. So Connor and I went ahead as Tia and Hannah and Maggie brought up the rear. We got to the bottom of the steps and Connor stopped. He was listening to what I'm not sure.

"Sarah, wait here with the others while I go up. I have a funny feeling." and off he went. Now that sort of scared me so I told the others when they walked up to me what he said. "Why? What's up?" Hannah whispered. "Not sure but a lot of stuff has happened lately. Maybe he just wants to be careful." I said.

"He's been gone a while, where is he? Maybe we should go up there." Tia whispered back clearly worried.
 "OK, well there are three of us and a dog. We can handle it." I said acting real brave which I wasn't. But I was sure we could handle most anything if we came as a number. As we started up he came to the top of the stairs.

"Someone tried to break in again Sarah. You two are coming home with us. I just called the police." "What? Again? Connor! What is going on?" I asked. "They set the alarm off, but not before they tried to cut the wires. They got scared off. They want in that house for some reason and knew you were gone. They must be watching." Now I was mad but still scared, and who is "they"? "Let's get you some clothes and wait for the police and we'll go back to my house."

He had that commanding voice that shot out directions and you just followed them. We went up the stairs and went in the house. Nothing was amiss but the porch door had been jimmied open. The alarm must have gone off and they left. We were just throwing clothes into a backpack when the police arrived.

Marjorie and Frank were right out front when they came. Odd. But maybe they were just nosy. I looked over to Sam's house next door but not one light was on. Was she gone? Did she see anything? The policeman seemed to know Connor and they talked in low voices out front before they came in the house.

He asked me a few general questions and said they would continue to patrol the street more frequently. We left the way we came, down the stairs. I said a silent prayer of thanks that no one was hurt or anything was stolen. I could hear my mom in my head saying you can replace material things but not lives.

We walked back down the beach with Hannah and Tia in front trying to figure out this mystery. I was quiet as Connor and I walked, wondering if I made the right decision to move here. I loved the house and the lake but not so sure with all of this going on. "Sorry you moved here?" he asked reading my mind.
"I was just wondering if I made the right decision." I said looking at him. "I'm glad you did." he said ever so softly I had to strain to hear it.

We reached the stairs to his house and walked up and sat on the patio. Tia made some coffee and brought out the pot. "I found some apple pie in the fridge and there's enough for all of us." she said proudly.

Hannah helped her get the plates and forks and we had pie and coffee around Connors patio table. It was still very warm out. He had turned on the lights around the patio. I had to admit I was still edgy. "Don't worry, you're safe here Sarah." he said as he turned some music on. Motown…my kind of tunes.

"I grew up with this remember Hannah? My parents were from the sixties and my mom loved Motown music. She used to dance with me when I was little in our living room."

I said suddenly missing my mom. "Sarah, she used to dance with both of us. We had so much fun with her." said Hannah laughing.

Connor had three bedrooms so Hannah and I took the one with the twin beds in it. One more day with my friend and tomorrow night she would fly out. I would miss her but I was having such a good time with her. We stayed up awhile and talked and there was a soft knock on the door.

Tia. She came in and sat on the end of my bed and the three of us talked and giggled until Connor said "Come on girls… you gona stay up all night?" "OK Dad…" Tia said as she got up.
She gave us hugs and turned towards the door. "I had such a good time with you guys, good night" she said as she closed our door and headed off to bed.

"I'm sorry all this happened while you were here Hannah." I said. "Oh, Sarah, it's exciting but now I'm gona worry about you. You stick close to Connor OK?" I just smiled. We were asleep in a few minutes.

Monday went by fast. We got up, had breakfast and went back to my house with Connor leading the way. He made a big deal of going in and looking around and then thumbs up. We all laughed. Hannah got packed and we helped Connor load up his truck with the grill. Tia drove it down as we walked. Then we all headed out in my jeep with Mags in the back to have a burger.

Hannah loved the burgers with the olives. We kept putting money in the jukebox and laughing all the while I was thinking about going home alone at night. Oh well, God would take care of me.
 I was sure of that even though I hadn't made up with HIM yet. I knew in my heart HE never left me.

We spent the afternoon browsing all the stores and boutiques and getting one last ice cream cone and then off to the airport. I didn't want to let Hannah go when we hugged and I know she felt the same way.

She waved as she walked in the gates and the three of us left. Tia was leaving in the morning to go back to Indian and her job, so that left Connor and me. We went back to my house after the airport and I made some coffee that we took out on the porch. We sat for a while and talked. After assuring Connor I would be OK, he and Tia went back to his house.

Locking up and setting my alarm, I went in, and got on my computer. I was curious as to who lived here before me. Would that have something to do with all the attempted break ins? I searched for my address. Nothing but my name came up. I decided to call Mrs. Lane and ask her.

"Before you dear? Well yes, it was Walter and Pat Gems. They were dear friends of mine. Walter passed away last year and Pat is in assisted living in St. Joseph. And actually if I remember correctly they were very friendly with the man who lived next door. Not where your Mr. and Mrs. Creepy live, but the other house. You know, the lady who wouldn't come to our party? Come to think of it I remember Pat telling me how, now what was his name, Gary, Greg no Craig. That's it, Craig, use to come over all the time and play cards with Walter and check in on them. Very caring fellow, she said. He spent a lot of time with them. Does that help you dear?"

"Yes! You don't remember this Craig's last name do you Mrs. Lane? Or what happened to him? Just getting some ideas for another book," I said, which wasn't a lie. I could use this all in another book that is if I lived to write it.

"Well, it was Craig something. Seems like he had a tree name. Not maple or sycamore." "Willow? Birch?" I asked. "Yes! That's it Sarah, Birch. Craig Birch. Lived there for about a year. Older man in his sixties. I never met him but Pat said he was so kind to them. I think he died in a car accident." "Thank you Mrs. Lane you've given me a lot of ideas. Talk soon."

I hung up and started searching for Craig Birch in St. Joseph, Michigan. Nothing. Then I searched Birch in Chicago. I figured I'd try all the surrounding cities. Bingo! Lawrence C. Birch. suspected mob ties with the Chicago Castelli family.

Could it be the same one? It didn't say his age but it did say there was no evidence tying him to any crimes the family was accused of. He must have relocated before their trial or after, as he was never mentioned again. Evidently the Castelli family was big news. I had never heard of them but I lived two thousand miles away in Montana. They were on trial for money laundering. What did that have to do with Mr. Lawrence C. or Craig Birch? Maybe he used his middle name when he moved up here. Did Samantha have any connection to Craig Birch? If he lived in her house. Maybe she was related to him. I never did get her last name.

I remembered the locket. I went to the bedroom and got it out of one of my shoes. Yes, I know my shoes; it's the mystery writer in me. Red shoes in fact. Shoes are a great hiding place.
 I looked at it when I went back out to my desk. The picture looked just like Sam. I turned it over. Nothing. Well I couldn't have everything.
 I made a note to go over there tomorrow and talk to her whether she wanted to or not. I was going to get to the bottom of this.

Chapter 15

The next morning Connor called early checking on me. I assured him all was well and to not worry. Then I took a long hot shower and made some jam and toast and took my plate and coffee out on the patio. I looked up to see Sam sitting on her patio. She glanced my way. "Sam, why don't you come over and join me for a cup of coffee. No one is here but me." I called over. Not sure why I said the last part but I wanted to reassure her it was OK. She just looked at me. "Come on, I'll meet you down at the bottom." I got up and just started walking toward the back. Hopefully she was too. I got to the bottom and glanced to my left to see her coming down. Good.

"I don't know Sarah," she said. "Come on up, it's just me and it will do you good to get out of that house for a while." I said as I turned and walked back up the stairs. Good, she was following. I went in and got another cup of coffee. "I made some toast and here's some jam."

I said as I pushed them toward her. She looked around the yard and then must have decided it was OK. She started eating. We sat and ate for a few minutes and listened to the lake. It gave me a moment to figure out how I was gona approach her. Well, why not just like she did? Point Blank. I just took a chance.

"Sam was your dad Lawrence Birch?" She stopped chewing and just stared at me. "I'm not trying to pry; I'm just trying to figure out why somebody keeps trying to break into this house. And I figured out who lived here and who lived in your house." Still nothing. She was chewing ever so slowly but looking at the table.

"Sarah, I'm sure I haven't lived the kind of life you have," she said quietly. I looked at her and took a sip of coffee before replying.

"I'm not so sure Sam. I've had a lot of tragedy in my life the last couple of years. Why do you think I moved here?

Now I have more problems. Someone is trying to break in or scare me off or have me move or whatever and I'm tired of it. I just want to figure it out. I thought maybe you could help me.

And I think this is yours. I found it on the floor in the living room." I slid the locket across the table. She touched it. "I thought I lost it and it's the only thing I have from him." she said quietly. Him? Her dad? I didn't reply. "I changed my last name from Birch to Hancock. I had to go to court to do it. I just was tired of being associated with the Family."

She looked up. "Castelli Family?" I asked. She nodded. "My uncles. My mother's brothers. She married my father when she was young. I don't think he had any idea what he was getting in to. She told me she wanted out, away from her family. But that's not the way it works Sarah. Family is Family."

"Well Sam, some are good some are not. You know what they say; we can choose our friends but not our family."

She just nodded. "I was close to my dad growing up. We had a good life I think. I know they tried to shield me from a lot. But then my mom got sick with breast cancer. It was a really bad couple of years and then she died. He was heartbroken. It was a very hard time for us. All we had was the family. And my uncles did care about my mom. My dad was a good man. He had his own accounting business, but the medical bills…. there were so many of them. I left as soon as I could after the funeral. I knew what their name stood for and I wanted no part of it.
My dad moved up here later. This was my grandparent's house. I think he just wanted to move away from it all and on one in the family knew about this place. My regret was that I didn't connect with him again."

She had tears in her eyes. "He was all I had. I moved to California for a couple of years and stayed with friends, but that didn't work out. When I finally decided to come back he was gone.

A car accident they said. I'm not so sure about the accident part. You don't leave the family."

"That's what I've heard. Is that why you're so scared?" I asked. She nodded. I can't imagine my uncles hurting me but my cousins would" she said pushing back her coffee.

"I can't stand them. My dad left me my grandparent's house along with a small trust fund. If it's them that's doing all of this, there must be a reason why. My trust fund is not that large at all." She looked at me.

"Mrs. Lane said your dad was close to Walt and Pat Gem who lived here. Said he was always here, kind of looking after them. Maybe that's where we start. Talk to Pat Gem. Mrs. Lane said Walt died last year but Pat is in St. Joseph in an assisted living facility. She might be able to tell you something about your dad. Are you game?"

I looked at her waiting. "OK." she said slowly, "yes, yes I am." "OK let's go. Let me call Mrs. Lane and see if she remembers which one." I placed a quick call to my friend who did remember it was Sunset View. We locked up the house and keyed in the numbers to the alarm. Off we went with Mags in the back seat. I was intent on finding something, anything, to figure this out. We drove into St. Joe and found it was located on the bluff. It had a huge fenced in patio and very nice accommodations.

We told the nurse at the desk we were old friends of the family and she led us to the patio. Mrs. Gen was sitting in a wheelchair watching the lake. "Mrs. Gem? Mrs. Lane told us you would be here. I'm Sarah and this is…" "Samantha! I would know you anywhere!" she exclaimed to our surprise. "Honey, where is your dad?" she turned in her wheelchair looking around. "He told me he would come see me and Walt. Where is Walt?" she asked. Sam and I looked at each other.

"Mrs. Gem, my dad isn't here right now. We just wanted to stop and see you for a few minutes. He sends his best though." Sam said leaning down and grasping her hand. Mrs. Gem smiled and then looked at her and mumbled something. "What did you say? I'm sorry I didn't hear it." Samantha said.

"Well Craig said he would come back and pick it up. We were to hold on to it just for a while. But he never came!!

Where is my Walter?" Mrs. Gem was clearly getting agitated. "Mrs. Gem, what did Craig give you? Where did you put it?" I asked frantic now for an answer. This must be what everyone was after. "Where is my Walter? Nurse! Where is Walter?" she yelled. The nurse came out with a frown on her face as she looked at us. "I'm afraid you will have to cut your visit short." she said as she bent down to calm her patient.

We left and I couldn't wait to get home. "There must be something in the house. Your dad must have left it with them. We need to tear my house apart." I said as I gripped the steering wheel. "That's a long shot Sarah. My dad has been dead for two years, and Mrs. Gem clearly has dementia or Alzheimer's. No telling if he did give them something if they even have it or kept it."

"Samantha, it's worth a try. What else do you have to do?" She nodded in agreement as we drove back.

We parked and got out only to have Mr. and Mrs. Creepy call to us from their front yard. Did these two just lay in wait? "Girls, girls how are you?" Frank asked. Marjorie as usual just bobbed her head. "Fine Frank, we're fine. Thanks for asking." I said and quickly opened the back gate and we went in.

"Those two are just weird Sarah" Sam said. "You think?" I replied and we started laughing. "I won't even start about his hair." we laughed some more. It was good to see Sam lighten up a little. "So where do we start?" she asked looking around the back yard. "Well let's start here in the yard first and work our way into the house. Think about a little old lady and where she would hide something."

We started in the shed and worked our way out. Nothing in there but dirt and pots shovels and rakes.

We walked around the yard and looked in the trees and under the picnic table, everywhere we could think. Finally, we headed to the house. "We go inch by inch." I stated.
 We keyed in the code and unlocked the back door. We went over the entire back porch looking in every nook and cranny. Nothing. "OK, let's stop and have lunch. I'm starving. I have stuff to make subs."

So we stopped and made giant subs and got a couple of cokes and sat on the patio. It was warm and breezy. "I wonder what he left with them?" Sam bit into her sandwich staring at the lake.

 "I don't know but he sure didn't want it on him or in your house. This would be the last place anyone would look. Two elderly neighbors. But somehow they found out. Or…maybe one of them visited Mrs. Gem and found out the same info we did." I said looking at her.

"You're probably right. If they found my dad and watched him for any length of time they would have seen him coming here. The house was pretty torn apart when I got here. I just thought some kids must have broken in and had a party. I was pretty edgy though, that's why I'm so leery of everything."

"Well Sam, I think we're both right. Something is clearly going on and I bet Mrs. Gem told someone the same thing she told us. So we are going to find whatever your dad hid."

We cleaned up the dishes and started in the kitchen. We literally took apart every cupboard and took out every dish. We took out the drawers and looked on the bottoms. We even moved the fridge out and looked behind. That was a mistake. I had to stop looking and clean. Nasty stuff is lurking behind fridges.

Then back to the hunt. My phone rang. I glanced down, it was Hannah. I'd call her back. We got up on the table and took down the glass globe on the overhead light. We looked everywhere. Broom closet, under the sink. We looked for any hidden compartments. None. We just looked at each other.

Next the dining room. It was actually part of the living room. But nothing was found. So we looked around the living room. We moved furniture back and then back again. We moved everything in that room. Went through the closet inch by inch. Nothing. We went through all the bookshelves, nothing. Little old lady I kept thinking. They were old and probably suspicious of everything. It had to be where she could reach it. But after hours of searching, we found nothing. We had searched the entire house. We were tired and disappointed as we sat on the couch at the end of the day and looked at each other.

"Nothing. I can't believe it. If your dad gave Walt and Pat something they would have hidden it here. I'm sure of it. We just can't find it. Want to stay for dinner?" I was very comfortable with Sam and glad to have the company.

"I think I'll go Sarah. Maybe I'll look through my dad's things and see if I can find anything." she said as she got up to go. "OK, well let me know. Sorry. I know it was a connection to your dad whatever it was he gave them." I walked her down the steps to the bottom of her steps and we said our goodbyes. It was still light out but dusk would be coming soon. I walked back up and stopped. There standing in my yard was Frank Bellows.

"Wondered where you were Missy" he said looking ridiculous but I was still weary of him. "What is it you want Frank?" I asked as I held Maggie's collar. Her growl warned him and he took a step back.

"Ah, well nothing really. Just wanted to know if you got any of our mail in your box. Waiting for something and never got it yet." he said as his eyes scanned the yard.

"Nope, can't say that I have Frank." I replied coldly. I did not like this man and neither did Maggie. "OK, well I'll be going." he said. I said nothing and just looked at him. He turned and went out the gate, and as he was closing it I let Maggie go. She stormed the gate barking. Good Hope he's scared.

I went back in the house and called Hannah back. She was settled back in her routine already and told me about the new hats she got in. We talked for about forty-five minutes and then I got off and made a salad. I knew I must be missing something. I just didn't know what it was. I locked up and turned on the alarm and hit it early. I was tired and didn't want to talk to anyone. Tomorrow would be better I assured myself.

Chapter 16

I got up around seven in the morning, which was late for me, and threw some sweat bottoms on. Puttering into the bathroom, I stopped. I was standing in water. Darn! A leak. Either the toilet or pipe under the sink. I dried my feet off and went and found my trusty pink toolbox.

Caleb bought it for me with the usual assortment of tools needed for repairs. Hammer, screwdrivers, nails, wrench, silver man tape, etc. Checking the area around the toilet and finding it dry, I cleared everything out from under the sink. I mopped up the water that collected there. Must be on the main pipe under there. This I knew how to do. I unscrewed the joint ring and tried to get the pipe off, but it wouldn't budge.

I tried harder and still nothing. I laid a towel down in the bottom of the cabinet and laid down on it on my back. Holding the flashlight to get a better view, I stopped. Frozen in place, I just stared. There it was. Taped to the bottom of the sink there was a small black book in what looked like a plastic bag. I just stared at it. I couldn't believe it. Here all the time. I reached up and pulled on it. Pat must have used half a roll of mailing tape as it was stuck pretty well. It must have been there for quite a while because I ended up getting a knife and cutting it to get it down.

I was quite careful as I took it out of the bag. Inside the front cover were the initials LCB. Lawrence Craig Birch, I was sure. There were names, dates and dollar amounts. Was this some kind of evidence against the Castelli Family? Did he have their money-laundering list? Is this what this was? Do I show Sam? Connor? As I sat there on the bathroom floor I suddenly didn't know who I could trust.

A loud knock on the door brought me back to reality. I stood up and stuck the book in the laundry hamper behind the bathroom door. I grabbed a sweatshirt from my bedroom and went to the back door. Maggie wasn't barking so I had a good idea of who it was. I was right. Connor. I keyed the alarm and let him in.

"Hey Sarah, how you doing?" he asked. "Just gona make coffee, want to stay?" "No thanks, just checking to see all is OK?" he asked looking at me. I didn't want to tell him about the book. "Yup, just getting ready for the day. I overslept." I lied again. O K God, maybe YOU could make some exceptions.

"Just wanted to let you know I'll be doing some paperwork at home most of the day but I will see you later OK? Please keep your phone by you today OK? I'll worry if you don't answer." he lingered at the door. "OK" I smiled. I watched him walk out and walk down the steps. Maybe there could be something there.

After making coffee, I turned around and went into the bedroom and was making the bed when there was another knock on the door. Maggie only barked once. I went back to the door and there stood Samantha. She looked at me through the screen. "I found it." was all I said.

She nodded and came in the door with some papers in her hands as I let Maggie out. "I found some stuff too Sarah. Hope I'm not too early." she said looking at my sweats. "No not at all. She taped it to the bottom of the bathroom sink. It was hard to see but I had a leaky pipe this morning is the only reason I found it.
I had to use a flashlight to even see it. What did you find?" I asked her.

She sat down at the table and smoothed out some papers. "Not sure. There are some dates and names of some of my uncles.
I'm not sure what any of it means though. It was in the middle of a family bible. Go figure. I didn't know my dad even read the bible." she said. I nodded. "I think we all call on God when we're in trouble. Maybe he found some comfort. Hold on."

I walked into the bathroom and reached down into the hamper and found the book. Walking back into the kitchen I saw she had poured two cups of coffee. I was really starting to like this woman. "Well I have sort of the same thing, names and dates, but there are also dollar amounts. What do you make of it?" I asked handing it to her and taking her papers.

"I'm not sure. I haven't been around my family for a long time. My mother never approved of her brother's "family business" as she used to say. She kept me pretty shielded. I just knew when I did see them I didn't like my cousins. They were forward and cocky. My dad had no use for them. Some of these names are my uncles. Tony and Louie. Most of the others are cousins and some names of their friends I think. They were a lot older than my mom." she continued to leaf through the book.

"Maybe he started writing them down on paper and thought a book must be easier to hide." I offered. "I don't know. I don't know what this stuff is. I know my uncle Tony and Louie were accused of being in bed, as they say, with the drug cartels. They have been in and out of court and jail for years. But they're both old now, in their late seventies. But my cousins aren't. I wouldn't put anything past them." she said with a scowl on her face. "Could this really be why you're having all this trouble?" she asked visibly concerned. "It has to be. But now I'm not sure what we do with it." I said looking at the papers and book. "Let me take a quick shower and get dressed and we'll decide. Help yourself to more coffee OK?"

I went into the bathroom and put the pipe back together. Repairing it would have to be done later. I took a quick shower and went into the bedroom. "Be out in a minute Sam." I yelled.

She didn't answer so I figured she was still going over the book. I threw some jeans on and a shirt and some tennis shoes. "Maybe we should consider showing Connor." I said as I walked into the living room and stopped.

"Maybe you should consider giving everything to me" said a red-faced Frank Bellow as he pointed a very large gun at Sam. He was huffing and puffing clearly out of breath. She sat in the chair with huge eyes staring at me. She mouthed I'm sorry. "What do you want Frank?" I asked him while my heart beat wildly in my chest. Why hadn't Maggie barked? "What do you mean what do I want?" he yelled. "I heard everything you said, even though I only had time to plant one bug in your bedroom. You had to walk in on us, before I could plant more. I want this book you're talking about! It must be worth some money to this Missy's family."

He was waving the gun around as it occurred to me Sam must have hidden the book. "You always were trouble. Couldn't keep your mouth shut could you Sarah? Had to blab all the time. You're responsible for our Adam!" he yelled as he waved the gun in the air. Adam! That's why Frank and Marjorie look familiar! They were his parents! I remembered them vaguely at the trial. They blamed me?? Adam murdered Caleb and Emily! How dare he blame me! I was angry and indignant. My phone started to ring. We all turned and looked at it on the couch. "Don't even think about it Missy." Frank said spitting venom I swear.

"If I don't answer it Connor will come here Frank. You remember Connor." I stated coldly. He stood there trying to figure out what to do. Suddenly the phone stopped. He looked relieved.
Then it started ringing again. If I could just keep him occupied maybe, we could get out of this mess. Come on God please intervene. "OK answer it. But don't say anything or I'll shoot her. "He threatened as he held the gun to Sam's head. "Hello?" I said knowing it was Connors number that showed on the screen.

"Sarah? Are you OK? I called and you didn't answer." he said.
"Connor, I told you I was going swimming today. I was just getting ready to head down. Can I talk to you later?" I lied again hoping God was truly on my side.

There was silence for just a few seconds then…" OK Sarah. I forgot. Bye." he stated very quietly. I hung up praying he got my message. "Where's Maggie Frank?" I asked hoping he didn't kill her and trying to stall.

"Don't worry about her Missy. No dog will pass up a good steak laced with sleeping pills." he hissed. "Now quit stalling and get the book" he said waving the gun around again.

"I have it in my bedroom." I lied and turned around as to go get it. "Stop right there! Where do you think you're going?" he asked. "You want the book Frank? I have to get it. Follow me if you want but it's in here." I lied. I knew I could defend myself physically from Frank, but I couldn't from a bullet. I started walking hoping he didn't shoot me. "Get up and follow her" he told Sam. She towered him by about a foot but I know she was so scared I didn't think I could count on her. I went into the bedroom and got my purse. I got my black address book out of it and held it. "Let her go Frank and I'll give you the book." I said trying to bargain, stalling. I knew it was useless.

"Give me the book Sarah and I promise I'll shoot you both." he said snarling. A knock on the front door stopped him. "Be quiet!" he hissed. The knocking wouldn't stop. "I have to answer it Frank. Whoever it is won't go away."
I whispered back. "No funny stuff!" he threatened. He followed me out as I went to the front door. He backed into the kitchen with Sam in front of him. He had the gun in her ribs.

I opened the door to Mrs. Lane and the pugs. Before I had time to do anything, she just opened the door and let those two snorting sneezing barking pugs in. I thought it was a bit odd for her.
Monty and Tilly came running in and went straight for Frank who started kicking at them.

Mrs. Lane reached in and pulled me through the front door with a forceful yank and I tumbled forward into the yard. I heard a shot. Sam!

I bust back through the door to find Sam sitting on the floor by the fridge and Connor standing over Frank with a gun! "You have the right to remain silent..." I couldn't believe what I was hearing! "Are you OK dear?" Mrs. Lane said behind me. I turned around shocked. "What? What's going on Mrs. Lane?" I turned back to hear Connor finish reading Frank his Miranda rights. Connor a policeman??? I stared at him. Shocked.

"Connor called me Sarah when he knew you were in trouble. I am what they call a diversion." she said looking quite proud of herself. "Connor came through the back porch and we saved you!" she said smiling. "Well my pug babies helped too! Didn't you guys?" she bent down to pet those snorting angels.

I just looked at Connor as he handcuffed Frank. He was on his cell phone and I heard a siren pull up. I helped Sam get to her feet. "You OK?" I asked. She just nodded and held tightly to my hand. Connor looked at me as two policemen led Frank away.

"Sorry Sarah. But the three of us need to talk." he said as he looked between Sam and me. "Connor I'm going to be going then." said Mrs. Lane as she hooked leashes to the collars of the pugs. "Call me anytime to help. It was quite exciting!" she said smiling as she walked out and started to close the front door.

"Thanks again Mrs. Lane." he called. I looked at him still bewildered. "Maggie's fine, he just fed her something to sleep. She's a little groggy but she's under her tree sleeping it off." I still just stared at him. He motioned for us to sit down.
  Sam was still pretty shaken up as he poured out our coffee and poured fresh into the cups. He poured himself a cup too. He looked at us. I waited.

"I don't really work for the power industry Sarah." "No duh" I said with a little bit of anger. "I'm a field agent for the FBI. I've been keeping an eye on Sam here." he said as he looked at her. "Me??" she exclaimed. "Well, not you in particular Sam. More like protecting you from your Family. But they've found you and they know your dad had the book. We're pretty sure they know he hid the book with the Gems. That's why all this stuff has been happening to you Sarah. Trying to get you out of the house and move even. Your new alarm gave them problems. We're sure they've already searched Sam's house.

They figured out the connection so you've been the target." He looked at me with what I was sure was pleading eyes. "Why the lies Connor?" I demanded. "The ONLY thing I lied about was my job. I couldn't take a chance on anything happening to you or Sam." he said. "What about Creepy Frank?" I asked.

"We ran him and his wife through our database and figured out who they were. What we didn't know is that they would follow you here after the trial. They moved just before you got here so they must have known your plans. I'm not sure what they were up to concerning you. But now we have them." he said softly.

So he knew. He knew about Caleb, Emily and the trial. He always knew. Liar. Then I was convicted, that still small voice from God telling you to forgive, nudging you into doing the right thing. I had been lying too, about a lot. But for now I was angry with him and in no hurry to forgive.

"So what now?" I asked coldly. "If we don't stop your cousins Sam, you're gona be running from them forever. Sarah and you are both in danger until we can catch them and prosecute. Your dad had a book listing the names, dates and amounts of money the Family was laundering from the drug business. He was on his way to meet one of our agents when they killed him." he said looking at Sam with sympathetic eyes.

"He was working with you??" she asked surprised. "Yes, he was. He had been for a while after your mom died. He was one of the good guys Sam, you can be proud of him." he said reaching over and squeezing her hand. She had tears in her eyes.

"We want to move you both and Maggie too, to a safe house till this is over," he said. "No way. No way Connor. "I said.
"I know that might sound crazy but I've been through hell the last couple of years and no one is gona run me out of my home now."

He looked at me, evidently figuring out it was useless to fight. "Well OK, but just plan on us being the three Musketeers from here on out till this is over. Sam you're moving in here until this is over if you refuse to go into hiding too." "If Sarah's staying, so am I." she looked at me for approval.

"Of course you're moving in. No discussion." I assured her. "I'll get your room ready and we'll get some of your clothes." "No, you'll get two rooms ready." Connor said looking directly at me. "No discussion." he stated. "You think you're moving in?" I asked acting as indignant as I could muster. "Yes" he said. He just stared at me. Somehow I knew better than to argue. "Fine." I said.

I got him the book of names and Sam gave him the papers she found. He made several phone calls and while we were at Sam's house getting her clothes, two agents stopped by my house to pick them up. I was still upset with him for lying but all in all, I was sort of glad to have him there. I felt a lot safer.

Chapter 17

I helped Sam get settled in the first guest room while Connor was making arrangements over the phone to have an expert come out and search the house for more bugs. I have to admit it was all a bit exciting and I had so many ideas for my next book. The problem with all of this was that it was real life. I was a bit scared.

I made lunch for the three of us and we visited around the table. Maggie was up and walking around with no after affects from the drugs so she was happy to have the attention from both of them. While we cleared the dishes the expert Connor called showed up to search the house.

He had some type of wand attached to a small machine and went through each room. "Your clean Connor." he stated. He left and we all look at each other. "Now what?" I asked. "Normal life. You do what you normally do." he said.

"Well, I normally write. How about you Sam?" I looked at her. "I'm good reading. Brought my kindle. I'll sit with you on the porch while you write." she offered.

The three of us moved outside. I wrote, Sam read and Connor worked on his laptop. It was actually a pleasant afternoon. He offered to grill that night so we all jumped in the jeep and went into town to the store. We bought some steaks, fresh asparagus and ingredients for a salad. We had fun in the store, joking around with each other. Sam was starting to relax and she was actually a lot of fun. I realized I really did like these two. A lot.

We bought ice cream and all the toppings so it looked to be a fun night. We stopped at Connors house on the way back and loaded the grill into his truck. He drove it down and unloaded it and then drove the truck back to his house, stating he didn't want anyone to know he was staying. He walked back on the beach. As far as anyone was concerned, he would leave that night.

Sam and I made the salad and asparagus while Connor grilled the steaks. It was a warm night with a slight breeze, just perfect for dinner on the patio. The steaks were delicious. We finished the salad and steaks and started to make sundaes. We laughed as we piled ice cream high into the dishes and added caramel, chocolate and nuts.

It was a nice ending to a really good dinner. It had been a long day with lots of excitement and Samantha wanted to turn in early. I couldn't blame her. I think I was still running on adrenalin.
We told her we would clean up over her protests and she finally agreed saying she wanted to take a hot bath and then to bed.

We washed dishes in silence and then out to the porch to sit on the swing for a while. It was dark out but you could see easily with all the stars in the sky. We laughed as we watched the lightning bugs and he told me how they use to put them in jars as kids and have lanterns.

He was comfortable. That was it. I remembered this same feeling; I had it with Caleb. For the first time remembering him didn't bring me to tears. "What are you thinking about Sarah?" he asked softly.

I turned and looked at him on the swing and realized he was a good man. Considerate, kind, and concerned. "I guess everything that happened today. What happened to Marjorie Bellows?" I asked suddenly remembering they lived right next door.

"Well, attempted murder comes with a high bond and she didn't seem to have it, so she's sitting at home and Frank in jail. Don't worry; I'm here so if she even thought of doing anything…" he didn't finish the sentence. "No, I'm not worried. It must have been terrible for them. I don't like either one of them but their son murdered two people and is on death row. I'm still not sure why they moved here."

"They didn't actually. They are only renting that house. She told our agents she was planning to go back to Montana to her sisters. Frank's not getting out anytime soon. "he said putting his arm on the back of the swing. I leaned back on it and stared up in the sky. God had gotten me out of yet another mess. I said my thanks to Him. I closed my eyes and after a few seconds I felt his lips on mine; soft and gentle. I kissed back and he drew me close to him. We sat for a long time on that swing saying nothing. It was a comfortable silence and nice end to the evening.

We turned in after locking up and setting the alarm. Lying in bed with Mags on the end snoring, I thought about the day's events. Frank Bellow. What a creep. Adam's parents, I thought they looked familiar, even with those ridiculous get ups. Plus, two people who I had grown to care about were staying with me. Maybe Mrs. Lane and my mom were right. Divine Appointments. Is this what this is God? A divine Appointment? I drifted off to sleep pondering that question.

I couldn't figure it out. Was I sleeping? What was going on? I woke up to a hand covering my mouth. "Sarah, don't say anything." Connor whispered close to my ear.
 I nodded my head and he removed his hand. Sam was right behind him on the floor, her eyes wide with terror. He pulled me down off the bed and motioned for us to get low. I could see the gun in his hand. He had Maggie next to him whispering to her to stay. She obeyed him.

I heard noise in the kitchen. Why hadn't the alarm gone off? My heart was pounding wildly in my chest. Again. Hadn't we already done this once today? Or was it the next day? I glanced over at the clock next to my bed. 2:46AM. I heard walking and muffled speaking. Connor got up motioning for us to stay and call for help.

He went and stood by the closed door, gun ready. I slid my cell phone off the nightstand and punched in 911. I said nothing to the operator and I knew they would automatically send a car. Probably two as Connors team was aware of the situation with us all in the house.

More muffled speaking and Maggie started her low growl. I stopped her; whispering for her to be still and she did. Connor opened the door ever so softly and started to go out. I frantically looked at Samantha. She also had a frantic look. I stood up, not sure of what help I could be but anything was better than nothing. I bent down and grabbed the golf club I kept under my bed and motioned for her to hold Maggie. I patted softly to the door and opened it. I could see Connor in the hall. I stayed back knowing he wouldn't be pleased if he saw me but if anything happened I was near enough and I would come out swinging!

Something did happen. Connor flipped on the lights and shots rang out! Maggie started barking as I heard someone being slammed against the wall and I ran out. It took a second for my eyes to be accustomed to the light.

A guy was lying on the floor and bleeding all over my living room carpet. It's amazing what goes through your head in these times. I'm thinking about my carpet, how will I get that stain out, and I turn to see some huge guy hold Connor to the ground hitting him. My cue. I swung and hit him hard in his head.

He fell like a ton of bricks. Connor looked at me as the front door was kicked in. Two agents came running in, guns drawn, yelling at me to put the club down. I just dropped it. Connor got up and took control of the situation. I started shaking as the shock started to set in. Maggie was still barking at the agents until I calmed her down. Samantha came out and identified her cousins.

They went to the hospital. I was hoping I didn't actually kill the big guy but I never wanted to see him again. Connor finished giving statements and the CSI took samples and pictures. Everyone finally left around six. I looked at the bloodstain on my carpet. "You can get new carpet Sarah." Sam commented as she stared at the spot. "I know; I think I will." I replied.

The two of us just stood looking at it when Connor came up behind us and put an arm around each of us. "What a day and a night." he said. "Let's get dressed and I'll take you ladies to breakfast at Tony's." "Great idea!" I said.

We took turns showering and got dressed. Maggie sat in the backseat with Samantha and we drove into town. The coffee was hot, strong and tasted great. Blueberry pancakes filled each of our plates as Connor filled Tony and Gabby in on the night's events. Sam was relieved after Connor told her that her cousins, if they both made it, would never see the light of day. I was happy watching Samantha laugh with Gabby and Connor and Tony talking about fishing. Divine Appointment God? Maybe, just maybe.

Epilogue

Everyone likes a happy ending tying up the loose ends. But life isn't always like that. The cousins did make it. Johnny, the one that was shot, is now paralyzed and in a wheel chair. He lives in a rest home. Nicky, who I clobbered with the club; well he's not quite the same anymore. He's living in a group home in Chicago. I feel bad when I think about it but not when I think of him trying to kill Connor. A life of crime doesn't seem to pay.

Marjorie Bellows went back to Montana after Frank was sent to prison. Revenge didn't work out. They were without their son and now without each other.

Samantha continues to live in her house. But now she comes out more. With her cousins gone, she doesn't have anyone to fear. She's working on her house and fixing her yard up and started going to church with Mrs. Lane. Seems Mark from church has a brother who seems quite interested in Sam to her delight.

Mrs. Lane still has her garden as well as her pugs, with one exception. Seems Monty and Tilly now have to share her with a new foster baby, another pug named Milly. Lots of snorting and kisses to Mrs. Lane's delight.

Connor is still with the FBI. We are dating. It's nice. It's comfortable. I will see where it takes us, this Divine Appointment. God is back in my life right where HE belongs, I guess HE never left. I'm still writing. Life has given me a lot of ideas for my books. Mom, I'm starting to dance again, and I'm not going to sit back as life happens anymore, I'm gona come out swinging!

Made in the USA
Middletown, DE
10 May 2016